An Instance of Opposition

R. Vincent Tibbetts

An Instance of Opposition

DEDICATION

To my father who somehow saw the writer in me.

ACKNOWLEDGEMENT

Writing can appear to be a very singular effort to the casual observer, however, it has been my personal experience that nothing could be further from the truth. My frequent interactions with friends and business associates has fostered an unbelievable amount inspiration and support for the projects I choose to take on. I am very grateful for their belief in what I am trying to achieve, or the care and kindness they have shown that has helped me complete this project—and this novel is no exception.

Listed below are the names of individuals who have had a hand, consciously or not, in seeing me to my goal:

The beautiful home and warm hospitality of Jim and Carrie Dussault located in the great state of Massachusetts. I am forever grateful for being invited to stay on this peaceful property, to occupy your guest house and take in the sublime energy of the surroundings to soak up the art and creativity found within. Although brief, I was able to explore some of Boston, MIT, and a few other areas mentioned in this book. I cannot think of one negative thing to say during my entire stay—except for those three hours we witnessed the Steelers take their usual shellacking in Gillette Stadium to open the 2015 season. The entire experience was beyond perfect, made a powerful impression on me, and was the answer I needed in putting this project together.

Stephanie Zapalac and her incredible company "Art of Life." Her continued belief in me, and the process of developing me as a creative entity has been unyielding. It has been a long journey of discovery, reflection, and adjustments to allow for the accomplishment of goals and the ability to realize my dreams. Some of those sessions have felt as clunky as an unrehearsed puppet show, and in others I have felt as tenuous as a marionette whose strings might not be connected quite right, but she has always been there with her Art of Life tool box to mend a heart or connect a string and guide me in what is important to following through with the show.

Stephanie has never failed to create a palette in which one is allowed to form color, define parameters, and produce a vision that allows for focus on what is needed to complete a project. Armed with dry erase boards, a fist full of purple cards, and just enough office fuel to navigate the week, she is your go-to when you need a go-to to go to. I have also come to believe Stephanie is the reason confetti balloons exist.

Naz Harounian and our fashion company of Sprezzatura Culture. By all accounts, Naz is a endlessly working, constantly thinking, driven, kind hearted, immensely creative, and exquisite soul. My partnership in business and long-lasting friendship has allowed me to share in her beautiful insights of life and be an observer to her artistic capabilities as her vision for things grow to become a reality in our company. There have been plenty of times our collaboration has felt as magical as a night filled with floating sky candles.

John Gasca and his continuing support for these projects and professional advice. His standard for exactness is only matched by his drive to be accomplished in whatever he undertakes. Thanks for the notes on the novel.

Michael Uribe and his continued support for these projects. It has been a long, long, road my friend. We should have left with a better map before we embarked in this crazy industry they call show business. One might be tempted to use the confetti balloon reference here, but alas it has already been taken.

Tanya and John Besmehn and their company of Bezuki Creative Services. This is the one-stop-shop for all of your editing and book needs. Creative covers, line editing, and advice are found within, and I am forever grateful for each and every project of mine that they have taken on and tackled. No easy feat I can assure you, but they are beyond being up to the task. I highly recommend you reach out to them if you are in need of anything related to publishing.

Finally, Jenee Rager and Al "Bullet" Burghard each, for your notes and insight. Thank you for reading and reporting back.

Every person listed here had a hand in creating this project, whether willingly or not, and I thank you.

Photo Credit: Naz Harouniar

Caelum Scalptorium: (Latin) the engravers' chisel

In the mid-eighteenth century, the French astronomer Nicolas Louis de Lacaille gave the southern constellation the French name Burin, (chisel) when translated back into Latin it ended up being Caelum Scalptorium. Respected astronomer John Herschel thought this name was too long for a constellation and suggested it be shortened to just Caelum, which is what finally came to represent the Chisel Constellation, but the word Caelum would also come to mean atmosphere, sky, or heaven.

CHAPTER ONE - TINDRA

Tindra sat in a lazy Zen like posture in the middle of her bed, legs crossed, her torso curved forward so that the only thing keeping her upright were the elbows she had poking out her dark oversized t-shirt and braced firmly against her bare knees. She stared at the blank page of her journal getting ready to write and if she had taken the time to look at her reflection in the mirror placed on top of her dresser across from the foot of her bed, she would have noticed how her legs matched the Manila pages of her journal. They, like the rest of her body, were toned and defined, but could never be described as muscular.

Her ankle sported a bandage marking her new tattoo. She had other works in ink, none were in color though, the one on her side was of a large dreamcatcher with the outer hoop on fire, a crawling tiger and slithering serpent were on the inner parts of her arms respectively, and now on her ankle, a freshly applied eyeball with no pupil and long exaggerated lashes that could have been mistaken for rays of the sun. These, along with her nose ring and ear piercings were there to accentuate who she was on the inside but failed miserably at muting her natural beauty or attributes.

Nothing could change the fact she had come from parents ill-equipped to raise a kid, adults who found ways of getting into more problems than they could get out of, and experienced the tail-end of a middle class that was left to sink in the rising waters of economic swells, of forceful ocean tides that would only allow for the largest of ships to remain afloat. Those choppy seas were the tempestuous economic driver leveraging people to the brink of poverty.

She knew well the feeling of disenchantment, it hung around like an older sibling, always there to smack her down when her hopes grew too high. Discouragement and discontent loomed because her parents cared more for each other than they cared for her, and she learned way too early in life that a person has to fight for the things they really wanted.

As most kids approach their teens, it is a time of fun, exploration, and promise, for Tindra it meant she became set in her ways, stubborn to the core, resisting anyone or anything that might box her in. Her teachers often described her as *sharp* when cornered with the task of describing her in a positive way. Otherwise, she was tolerated.

This bleak compliment lit a fire in her belly until she ultimately discovered the magic of putting pen to paper and the glorious release in writing. From that point on, she wrote almost every day of her life, relishing a welcome release in finding the conversations in her head a home on a page. Ever since she could remember, there was dialog taking place inside her mind—a pandemonium laced theater of the absurd, and she desperately needed a platform in which to purge those thoughts.

Writing became the tool to her mounting internal struggles, of toeing the line, of maintaining a calming front amid the constant siege of madness. This steadfast anger percolated inside her, looking for a release, and it needed to be expressed in a meaningful way. This wasn't always possible, sometimes she had to eat it like she was trying to eat her own fist. After having to do that more times than she cared to admit, she took comfort in the throes of isolation.

Tindra often envisioned herself screaming into the faces of the parents that had abandoned her in the name of narcissism, or any other type of parental authority that wished to fill their shoes. She was a spirited young woman, attracted to the steamy edge of punk, piercings, and the dark, permanent ink of tattoos, and with each passing day was coming to grips with the fact she would always be a loner.

This vengeful angst did little to improve her life, but it wasn't always about life improvement, sometimes it was about the energy building inside her looking for a release. She found no substitute for putting pen to page, and it wasn't like she didn't try. She was well aware that kids her age found their release in throwing rocks through windows of abandoned buildings, taking a bat to side-mounted mirrors of parked cars, setting fires to dumpsters after the nighthawks had scrounged for leftovers from the plates of the elite. She'd joined them once or twice but that kind of destruction did little in making her feel good, in fact, it made her feel guilty. She found no joy in getting away with this type of vandalism because she found she couldn't escape herself.

The only instrument available to her was the act of writing. There was an undeniable power to the written word, she could see it, read it, and revisit it any time she wanted. At times a sentence or paragraph framed her feelings so well that it became a snapshot for her state of mind, and was the very reason she kept writing entries into her journal.

The school they deposited her in, before her parents pulled their vanishing act, viewed her as she viewed them — a disappointment. The minimal interest any teacher showed in her revolved around the one shining capability she came to possess, for her it was effortless, but they kept harping her on it, pointing it out until she could have cared less about developing it any further, especially if it meant impressing them.

Typing incredibly fast came naturally for Tindra. Her teachers kept trying to push her toward careers that would exploit this skill, but those jobs sounded frightfully mundane or subservient. She refused any possibility of seeing herself sitting in a courtroom employed as a stenographer, nor did she see herself as a secretary, or with any job that required her to perform a concise edit to something already written. Those weren't careers that appealed to her, nothing that structured ever would. Tindra had an endless desire for change. Doing the same job day in and day out would have driven her bonkers.

This was one of the aspects that made going to school so difficult for her, the other being the teachers that were trying to push her toward a mental breakdown. Whether purposeful or not, pushing her towards careers she had no interest in made her sick to her stomach. When they finally took a break from it, her classmates had no problem picking up the slack in trying to drive her over the edge. In their own cruel way they decided to label her a freak, and not just because of her insane ability, she also stood out by dressing differently from the other students. She found comfort cloaked in darker colors, and these style choices seemed to make it abundantly clear to them that she was headed to a life that wouldn't require the furthering of any kind of book knowledge.

This was how Tindra found herself going from loner to outcast, and graduated to this with honors, always acting the part. She would show up late for class, or failed to complete a homework assignment in protest, of course to her teachers' expectations. As time went on, everyone easily fell into their roles, she refused to engage in any assignment she found to be boring or

5

beneath her, and in turn. her instructors would turn a blind eye to what she hadn't done or find something she would take an interest in and complete. They were passing her to get rid of her, and she was playing along to get rid of them.

A game, that's what life was becoming for her, a game she would want to win, and on her terms. In that vein, typing words out onto a page at blinding speed felt more like a gimmick than a gift, and that was how she embraced it. One day it occurred to her to merge the two. If she wasn't going to do her homework, then she could do the homework of others. Tindra turned her blazing finger speed into profit by offering to type her fellow students' papers. Her services weren't advertised, keeping things on the down-low was how she flew. Her in was discovering not every honor student acted with honor. She found dealing with this small group was the best way for her anonymity to remain intact. They, of course, wanted to keep their dealings with her a secret, so as not to tarnish the reputations of brilliance they were trying to cultivate. Typing for profit was what kept her interest going and for staying in school for as long as she did. All the while, Tindra was learning and retaining the things she wrote, which made her acing a test all the more perplexing to her teachers.

Graduating high school was never going to happen in a timely fashion, not with her skirting the narrow boundaries of passing or failing each year, she may have aced her tests, but she would receive incompletions for work not turned in. It became a game of manipulating the system, and as the time for diplomas approached and the threats of holding her back one more year surfaced, Tindra simply dropped out. Even if she did earn her diploma, she would have never picked it up, let alone participate in their silly ceremony. In the end, she felt no real connection with the physical presence of the place, nor with any of the students, so when she decided to bail, she never had a reason to look back. She wandered for little over a year holding part-time jobs at a laundromat, a video rental store, and then at an independent coffeehouse.

Out of all those jobs she wanted to like, the video rental store looked to be the best because she was able to keep up with the latest movies, but that got old fast as the trailers they played in house were on a loop, and after four hours of hearing the same sound bites over and over again she wanted to shoot herself in the head. The coffeehouse turned out to be the real winner and seemed like a better match to her personality. The individuals that came by were eclectic, always busy doing something constructive, even if they were planning just to have fun. Then there was the drink making, treats like a dirty chai tea latte, a Keith Richards, an Espresso, or a Ristretto meant she was getting paid to create things people wanted and more often than not, appreciated. She was personable because that was how she made her tips, but that was about as far as Tindra would allow anyone in. She was much more content being a people-watcher than a participant.

One day while taking orders, she ran into an honor student she used to type papers for, a guy named Nicolas Prin. He was tall with blonde hair, broad shoulders, and a smile that naturally showed anyone, who might care, that he had everything under control. It was an awkward moment for Tindra, and she hoped it would pass quickly. There really wasn't anything for them to reminisce about, but that didn't stop him from hanging around waiting to speak with her. As soon as she was able to go on break, she made her way over to his table.

"What do you want?"

"Tindra, that isn't the way two classmates should speak with each other."

"I have fifteen minutes and don't wish to spend them all talking with you."

"Well, I see not much has changed with you since you left high school; still, I am in a unique position to offer you a job, if you are so inclined."

"Doing your homework again?'

"Come on, you weren't doing my homework, I have very little time to type out my assignments, both then and now."

Tindra was unenthused by his presentation. She started to make her move to escape, but Nicolas quickly reached out and grabbed her arm.

"I admit you helped more than I realized, I reread some of those papers and you added quite a lot of content, rounding out what was needed for the assignment to perfection, of course."

"It was all in the books they assigned. You should have tried reading them a little more thoroughly yourself."

"Agreed. I found myself torn between subjects I was really fascinated with, and the subjects I needed to get a good grade in but couldn't put in the work. I'm sure playing athletics didn't help much with my time allotment."

"We all make our own beds." Tindra tried to break away, but Nicolas wouldn't let her go. Tindra was not pleased with how she was being treated and shot him a stern look.

"I need your magic again Tindra, it will be different this time, my notes are much more extensive, but then again, so are the assignments. I still don't have time to type…"

"They don't have people at that school who type?"

"No, they do. They do. It's just that most are indisposed, they have plenty of clients and do an exact job. Too exact of a job. I could use someone like you, with your skill sets for writing, plus I would have an advantage over the other students because I would have you all to myself."

"This is a paid position?"

"Yes, but there is one catch, you would have to move where I am going to school right now."

"And where would that be?"

"Massachusetts. I'm enrolled at M.I.T."

"It's cold there."

"Well, yes, during the winter..."

"I don't particularly like the cold."

"It's not cold year-round."

Tindra looked at him unmoved.

"I will get you a jacket."

She didn't blink an eye. Nicolas leaned in closer to her.

"I will pay you more than what you make here ..."

She stared at him for a moment as if to question his sincerity. Breaking free of his grip, she grabbed a napkin from a table and pulled a pen from her apron pocket. She scribbled on the napkin, then shove it in front of him, "That's twice what I make here and the price I would need to consider such a move."

Nicolas looked at the napkin and noticeably squirmed, Tindra turned on her heel as Nicholas called after her.

"Okay, okay. It's a deal."

Tindra stopped, then slowly made her way back toward Nicolas. His hand was extended as if to shake on it, but Tindra refused. She had one more demand, "I will need a place to stay—a place of my own, which means I might need first and last on the rent. I would expect to get this as an advance when I find the place I like."

Nicolas withdrew his hand as he thought about what she had said, he didn't completely pull it away and several seconds later he extended it again. Tindra reached out and shook it. Without saying a word, she turned and walked away, Nicolas frowned as he called after her.

"Hey, don't you want to know when to come or how you can reach me?"

She continued walking as she shouted out loud enough for all to hear, "Knowing you, I assume it's as soon as I can, which means I will get there when I can get there, and at that point I will find you. The kid whose parents pay for everything."

Nicolas sat stunned. He was hesitant to leave, analyzing if he had made a mistake. Her work was impeccable though, and she had no problem hanging under the radar, which was exactly what he wanted. There was little else he could do but laugh to himself, she had that edge of wanting to find things out on her own, so of course, their conversation would end this way. He grabbed his coffee and headed for the door.

This was how Tindra came to live on the outskirts of Cambridge.

The papers Nicolas needed for his M.I.T. classes were far different from anything she had drafted in high school. There was a leniency the professors refused to show in grading a paper that a high school teacher might let slide. There was no mercy found on this academic landscape, they continually pushed for excellence out of their students, and Tindra, like the others, had no problem keeping warm by the fires of that competitive torch.

She would get the parameters for each assignment, making sure she paid special attention to specific instructions. She would grab a copy of the book and read it from cover to cover highlighting important facts along the way. As soon as she was finished, she would begin typing out the assignment. She would review the notes Nicolas took and compare them for any insight he might have gleaned outside of what she had already done. More often than not, there was little if anything new he had to offer and Tindra would then churn out a clean, clear, and concise paper.

There was a learning curve for the work she was doing, such as going to the student bookstore to find a particular edition of a used book because it still had a section that wasn't redacted in a newer copy. When going to the library she taught herself how to fill out the forms so she could request a volume, even if it meant transferring that volume from another library, and if the book happened to be checked out for an extended period of time, she also learned how to track that student down. It was in this atmosphere she trained herself for a future in doggedly retrieving the facts.

THE BASEMENT ON BEACON HILL

The great change forecasted in government by many political pundits was taking effect. Deregulation spread from business models to social services and, America as the Great Society began to vanish. It wasn't anything a person could readily see as the administration rolled out its new proposals and implemented their policies, but as time passed one could go back to the day the country stopped caring for its own, began shipping jobs overseas, and lost its luster. That is what it looks like when a political party plunders a nation for its wealth. Tindra would look back and remember it as the year she moved to Boston.

When she arrived in the Bay State, it was with the intent of doing her best to try and tone down the chip she had on her shoulder. She felt the change would do her good in accomplishing this and wanted to take advantage of her new start. This renewal of her being was one of the main themes for graduating to these parts.

Getting a feel for life in Boston quickly tested one's sense of loyalty. The inhabitants were brash about their love for this city, and you were either with them or against them in this line of thought. There wasn't much of a grey area for this and they weren't afraid to call you out on it. This attitude was topped off by the cultural vibe emanating from the surrounding universities and renowned institutions. This aura of high standards and intellect was awash in the quaintest of boutiques, upscale delis, fine restaurants, and countless shops that peddled goods and services. These establishments took on themes for artistic creativity, supreme quality, and high-end goods and services, this was because they also overlapped with the monetary wheeling and dealings within the High Spine of Back Bay. The financial success from those city blocks didn't just spire into the air with the construction of their towers and skyscrapers, it peppered the nearby neighborhoods with value and wealth. The people immersed in this influential district began to expect the best, and their best became the city's best. These expectations carried over from their business transactions to a night out on the town, from their personal dealings and affairs to their sports teams. Expecting the best, being around the best, meant one was in-the-know and the inhabitants carried themselves with a great sense of pride. The bustle that was the comings and goings of everyday people of the city, coming to experience the flavor and forward thinking that was Boston was what had William Tudor referring to Beantown as the Athens of America, and Tindra found herself swimming in this reputation as it converged, percolated, and bubbled over the city on the hill.

Cambridge Port was by far the first and most logical location she looked for a dwelling, but the neighborhood was going through a period of renovation and rezoning. For all the positives this might have had on the neighborhood, the flurry of activity and construction would have dampened Tindra's spirits, but not as much as the thought of having one of her clients unexpectedly stopping by her place. The close proximity to MIT gave this idea an all too real possibility and closed any hopes for her staying in this neighborhood. She took her housing search across the Charles River.

As she traveled over the Harvard Bridge by bus, she noticed the people riding their bikes and it made an impact on her, they were free to go where they wanted to, content with who they were and what they were doing, and more importantly they looked to have a purpose in this life. Tindra wanted that feeling of purpose and could see herself riding a bike around town; so, the first thing she did was buy herself a second hand bicycle, and thoroughly investigate the neighborhoods on the other side of those banks. Back Bay was out of the question, even with the ransom she was asking from Nicolas the rents were far out of reach. Peddling just a little further around town she passed through Fenway Kenmore, Bay Village, Lower Roxbury, and South End until she rode into the neighborhood of Beacon Hill. This area was far enough away where she felt she wouldn't be bothered by someone swinging by for a surprise visit, but close enough that she could still ride her bike, or take the bus in more inclement weather, when she needed to get back over to Cambridge.

Beacon Hill was built like most swatches of Boston from the razing of nearby hills to fill in its shoreline and bodies of water such as ponds or saltwater marshes. The solid brick construction of row houses, pair houses, and mansions were a direct reflection of the fire codes from the 1800s, with the residents being almost on top of each other, a structure fire carried the threat of wiping out an entire city block.

Tindra wandered the tight-knit neighborhood and couldn't help but notice all the black and white national flags hanging from the houses as if the owners of those contrasting colors were trying to recapture the national pride one used to feel for the country. She wondered how many of those residents were hanging their flags out of fear.

The neighborhood was blanketed with sidewalks precisely laid of brick, some butted up against black wrought iron fences meant to defend what small real estate had been measured out between the building and thoroughfare. There were stunningly trimmed storefronts to buildings that jetted up until they became the cozy tiers of residential dwellings. Of trees and foliage that seemed to instinctively know to compliment the man-made terrain of paved and cobblestone road. These things married themselves together and conjured up images of a time when the great city of Boston first began.

Sometimes she walked the blocks of this colonial neighborhood, the quarter seemed to uniformly grow until it towered over her, carving away large portions of the skyline. She found it easy to get lost in the feeling of stateliness as she was swallowed up by the rows of manors and mansions. These structures crisscrossed each other with a vibrancy for proper living and refined tradition. It caused Tindra to stop at times to take it all in, and she wanted nothing more than to be able to call one of these houses home.

As she cycled through Beacon Hill she came upon the beautifully trimmed fields of Boston Common, and there on the spot began falling in love. The red maples and honey locusts were just beginning to turn with the arrival of fall. Their orange, red, and yellow hues were undeniably magic, adding to the enchantment of the city, and she gravitated toward their radiant display. These resplendent colors also meant that the new semester was rapidly approaching. The dwellings in the surrounding area followed this flow of change, with one day being available, and the next occupied with an unripe freshman laden with a backpack and hope.

Tindra had come into town unannounced because she wanted to get a feel for the city without being pressured to remain. There was always the chance she might not like where she was at, or that things wouldn't feel quite right about the move, but none of those situations manifested themselves, it was now time for her to take the next step.

Staying at the small hotel, she was coming to the realization that her money would soon be running out, maybe she could hold out for a few more weeks before it all came crashing down, but why wait for that. Knowing what a first and last looked like for an apartment, plus what she would need to make ends meet until she started to get paid was what she would seek. It wasn't hard to find Nicolas Prin, she had a sneaking suspicion he might continue following through with his athletic endeavors, and so once on campus, she found her way to the Alumni Pool, or as it was more commonly known on campus, building fifty-seven. Through some snooping, she was able to find results posted for athletic events held there, and because of this was able to deduce he was still participating in swim meets. With a little direction from the kindness of strangers, she found herself walking to Albany street, heading southwest to the Ashdown and the newly renovated Next House.

As she strolled around campus she began to notice a difference between herself and the student body. It wasn't a bad thing, she wasn't ashamed of who she was, but she could feel the difference. It had to do more with tone than with style, more with confidence than cockiness, it laid in what one knew and what they believed. This confidence made them comfortable enough to let their guard down, to get lost in their thoughts, get to a truth that was deeper than any political belief, a truth that was rooted in the very foundation of the universe. That energy permeated throughout the dorms, reverberated in the halls, and were reflected in their sculptures, until it took hold of the campus submerging into one gigantic think tank.

Tindra wasn't sure she had that quality, she had a problem with letting her guard down, and that translated into mistrust. She came off to most as being cold, then there were those who saw her as being indifferent and those who misread her attitude entirely as having a superiority complex. The truth be told Tindra was just trying to put distance between herself and those around her. The world was populated, on the verge of becoming overpopulated, or at least that was how the news outlets seemed to be going out of their way to make everyone feel. It was as if they were trying to prepare their subscribers for the onslaught of disease, starvation, the unending flow of a migrant population that would overrun their lives, and the unavoidable zombie apocalypse that would soon follow because of it. If she were to somehow be admitted here, having to attend school and go to classes, she would've had her days of being out of place, of standing in the middle of a courtyard with a thousand yard stare and looking as if she were holding a grenade, a finger through the metal loop always at the ready to pull the pin. The pressure for having to let her guard down would have taken its toll. It wasn't like she hated educational institutions, not like the government hated them. The *elite intellectual* label seemed to cater to those who didn't go to college, hated being talked down to by those who did, and hated that the facts scientists and educators touted didn't sync to their way of thinking. There were a lot of facts not marrying up to a lot of beliefs, so there was a lot of hate to go around.

Tindra didn't like educational institutions because she had a huge distrust for authority. She wanted nothing to do with the regiment, or to sit in class listening to a professor drone on about the book he wrote for the class that every student was required to purchase. The only way she was getting near a college was if someone paid her. *Hello, Nicolas Prin.*

Her forthcoming, unannounced visit with Nicolas' did not have her feeling good at all about knocking on his door. She anticipated an uncomfortable terse greeting, followed by her request for cash. Even though her visit would be based on business they agreed upon, arriving unannounced violated one of her core beliefs, and she was having a difficult time embracing the transgression. Before she knew it, she was rapping her knuckles against the wooden door, and when it opened, all her fears were confirmed. Nicolas opened it wide to reveal the dorm room in a cozy state, complete with mood lighting, low playing music, and a female study companion.

His intension may have been to show whoever was on the other side he was otherwise engaged, but his demeanor changed at the sight of Tindra, and he slowly closed the door behind him.

"Tindra, what a pleasant surprise."

"I didn't know what else to do, I think I may have found a place in town to stay and I need your help."

"To move?" Nicolas looked a little perplexed, he had no intention of helping her with moving her stuff.

"Not to move," her face flushed with frustration. "With the process of completing the transaction." She made a small hand gesture as if she were signing a check. Nicolas picked up on Tindra's clue. It forced his tongue against the inside of his cheek as he contemplated a response.

"Ahhh, I'm not in the position to make that happen at the moment..."

"When will you be in position?"

He ran his hand through his hair. "I don't know..."

"Look, I'm sure you want to get back to your company."

"Yes, yes, you're right. Let's meet tomorrow morning, the coffee shop, Beantown, say at eleven."

"And you'll have the money?"

"How much?"

Tindra reached for his hand, opened it, and wrote a number on his palm. "That will cover the first and last plus expenses."

Nicolas processed the request, "I'll...we'll work it out."

She looked at him skeptically.

Nicolas tried to ease her fears, "I'll make it happen, for sure."

"See you there."

Tindra turned and was out before he could change his mind.

Off of the causeway in the middle of Beacon Hill there was a mansion that had been built at the turn of the century and converted to an apartment complex. It had five very spacious floors that had been remodeled so that each floor had two units that were totally self-contained. Upon entering the building, Tindra was immediately put off by the entryway, it would most certainly have her running into one of the other tenants living there. She would have turned around right then if the supervisor hadn't opened a door that lead to the basement. Following the long straight staircase, she passed through a second door and found herself in what used to be the servant quarters. It was beautifully laid out and took up the entire lower level, every room she looked at, every space she examined had her mind racing as to what she could do with it if she lived there. It was more than enough for any single person, and with every step she took she began to feel more and more comfortable in this space.

No one would find her down there, she felt protected from the outside world and could happily stay hidden for days, and if she ever wanted to leave without being seen, she was the only tenant with a backdoor. What pushed her over the edge and had her showing up to Nicolas' dorm room unannounced was the large fireplace in the back bedroom.

The smell of coffee was always a welcome sensation for Tindra. She didn't realize how much she enjoyed the aroma until she quit the coffee shop she had worked at back home. Now, every time she wandered into a venue serving caffeine in this dark, beautifully warm form, she melted with a simple internal joy. There were times she would find contentment in just holding the warm cup in her hands, taking in its rich redolence.

It was how she found herself sitting at a small table within Beantown, waiting for Nicolas. He was running late as usual and instead of getting caught up in his bad planning Tindra chose to find patience through her Zen-like coffee state.

When she did his papers in high-school Nicolas would brag to her about how much his family was worth, not his immediate family, but his grandparents. They owned a perfume company that had quietly bought one or two other name brands. The business transactions were seamless to the public, once acquired they never changed the formula, or the labels, or anything that would disturb brand recognition. They simply bought them and made sure they always wound up on a shelf in a department store or marketplace. Over the decades, their strategy paid off, and the grandparents had amassed a very large sum of money. So large that the grandfather had started his very own privately-run car museum. He had automobiles from all over the world, some were one of a kind, and to anyone interested in conveyances such as these it was utterly fascinating.

What more than fascinated Tindra back then was the deathwatch Nicolas had for his grandparents, he constantly said things like, *when they are gone, and after they die*. It was a horrible way of looking at anyone while they were living, let alone for the sole purpose of capitalizing on their wealth.

It was rumored when they had family get-togethers or the matriarchs would come for a visit, Nicolas would find a way to spend the least amount of time with them, but on the other hand, he couldn't wait for the day he would take advantage of everything they had ever earned.

So, it was after their passing, Nicolas' parents got a divorce. Each had enough money to start their lives over again but didn't want their significant other to be around to share in this rebirth. For Tindra this only confirmed Nicolas was of the same cruddy mold as they were.

Their split was the final safeguard toppling over in Nicolas' life. There was nothing stopping him now from becoming just another spoiled rich kid, getting whatever he wanted, whenever he wanted.

If Nicolas had a tail when he walked into Beantown, it would have been between his legs. His wet hair slicked back, he wore a loose-fitting sweat suit which had him looking as if he had just rolled out of bed. He may have done just that. He placed the check on the table in front of Tindra, she caught a glimpse of the smudged number on his palm. She Smiled. Nicolas assumed the smile was because she had been paid, but nothing could have been further from the truth. Her smile was there because he had transposed the first two digits written on his palm, instead of fifty-seven, he had given her seventy-five.

There was a sweet irony in this error, given their close proximity to an institution that got all it could out of every number used in a formula or proof. Boy, had Nicolas Prin found a long rope to hang himself with. Tindra pictured him dangling on that rope as he tried to prove exactly how he got into the university to begin with. His grades weren't up to the standard expected of a student applicant. Was there ever really a scholarship set aside for him? No doubt there would be talk around campus that his parents paid for him to be there. If that fact proved true, Tindra would have been the least surprised.

It seemed every year the wealthy were going out of their way to prove to everyone that the laws weren't written for them. They expected everyone else to play by those rules while they just bought their way out. It was the same attitude they had about paying someone for a service, they acted as if the transaction meant they owned that person.

Tindra vowed a long time ago never to let anyone hold that kind of power over her. It was one reason why she would never tell Nicolas where she resided. She didn't think anyone would ever find her down there, so she put a first and last down on the apartment with the fireplace as soon as the check cleared.

For the first time in her life, Tindra found a place she could really call home.

CHAPTER TWO – CLIVE

In the past, Clive never had to battle the negative feelings he had for his job. He had been warned back at the Academy days like this might happen for him if he exhibited sympathetic behavior toward the population when out in the field. Once deployed in a theater of action they were told it wouldn't end pretty for any of them if they began to feel even a hint of compassion for those they were there to persuade, police, and control. There wasn't a gauge or a warning light that would go on at some panel back at operations if a violation like this were to occur. It was rumored that for any agent displaying such feelings, there would be little choice but for them to go on the run, and in fact, those in charge expected it. There would be that day an operative wouldn't show up for an assignment or refuse to return a page. They wouldn't be found at one of the many safehouses or come in out of the cold when extended the offer. No, when they turned their backs on the system, they left the agency with one option and one option only, and the agency would come after them with everything they had to hunt them down.

They boasted of always getting their man. The agency wasn't talking about the criminals they had been hired to apprehend, they were talking about the termination of their own. Two boards hung at the main hall of their headquarters. At one end of the hall was a board with the list of names for all of those who were ever killed in the line of duty. It was a place of honor that signified the ultimate sacrifice an agent had given in upholding the rule of law and the way of life the government promoted and prescribed. Far away and at the other end of the hall was another board where they listed the names of agents who were killed while trying to escape. Both areas in that building were solemn places, purposely constructed for reflection, although one didn't find too many people hanging out in the area reading the names of those who ran, that kind of reflection happened at home, at the local bar, or in the haste of packing their bags to attempt an escape.

It didn't take much to convince Clive that it was a small world. It was a small world because there were no space stations or hubs orbiting high above for tourists to go and get away, no off-world colonies an individual could go and start anew. It was a small world because with each passing day his agency was gaining insight on how to better track individual people. Those outside the borders were steadily refusing to comply with anything asked of them by this nation of might, even if threatened, and so it got smaller because one by one these nations began to band together.

Even with like minds running the country the leadership seemed to be in chaos, the global agenda it was pushing was being rejected at every turn. However, just because countries on the outside hated this nation, it didn't necessarily mean they hated its citizens, in truth they actually felt sorry for them. They wanted nothing more than to reach in and remove the blindfold from their eyes. To wake every person up feeding on the steady diet of falsehoods the administration espoused, the unmasking would have revealed a world its citizens knew nothing about. They were told the rest of the world was an evil place, that those outside the borders had stolen their jobs, and if given the chance, wanted nothing more than to destroy their way of life.

Clive may not have been the smartest guy on the planet, he knew there were pockets of radical ideologies out there that sought the destruction of everything and everyone around them, but they were known and they were the minority. He knew for this country to survive they needed allies, they needed fair trade agreements, and they needed to be more understanding to the pain and suffering that was going on in the under developed areas of this world. Clive had been around, he had seen these war torn cities and slums, the people there really needed help, but whether or not this assistance would happen was a completely different story. The government may have indeed had fair trade agreements, were helping people in disaster zones and were part of a united front against terror, but no one knew this because no one in those positions of power ever talked about it. What the government did talk about was that the country needed no one to survive, didn't depend on goods or services outside of its borders, and would engage in conflicts all over the globe, anywhere the enemy chose to rear its ugly head, and there were a lot of enemies.

Clive also knew as a government agent he wasn't welcome beyond these borders, any government worker trying to defect wouldn't last long once their cover was blown. People like himself would be accused of being an operative, or a spy trying to blend into that society. Governments outside of this country began to believe there was no agent that actually wanted to defect, there always had to be an ulterior motive as to why they showed up on foreign soil. This line of thought happened because of the stench cast upon these government employees, everyone outside the agency believed they would be loyal to the end. The Agency had no problem using dirty tricks, especially against one of their own if they got out of line. Eventually, an operative got used to spending the better part of an assignment, a mission, even the rest of their life looking over their shoulder.

His focus for now was on something else that was unwanted for a long time, but now entering his life—a bottle of bourbon on his coffee table. The purchase of it was a first, and he contemplated whether or not to even open it. Every mission would have its hitches, the bumps in the road that caused one to question the need to follow through with it. For the most part, Clive was able to quiet the things that caused him to question a mission, this latest one, however, was different.

He had set the device in the Bronco earlier that day while their target was at work. It was a remote-control device that would cause the vehicle to stall when Clive punched a button on the controller. The timing for this was crucial if they were to get the desired effect the mission called for.

The government needed to convince the people to give up on their gas guzzling cars in favor of smaller, newer, greener cars. They were being sold as better for the environment, with higher safety standards, and less reliance on gasoline. These were all true facts, but what the government wasn't telling the consumers was that the agencies responsible for safeguarding the country were also able to track the newer automobiles with ease through a deal struck with the manufacturers to install surveillance hardware into each vehicle's system.

To gain the buy-in they desired by its citizens, the government began reporting that the newly refined fuel being sold at gas stations across the country would cause older models to stall out with no advanced warning. They staged incidents that were aired by news outlets with stranded motorists complaining about being stuck out in the middle of nowhere. Once enough of those stories trended, they began to carefully choose people with older model vehicles, planting devices in them that would cause these modes of transportation to stall at the most inopportune times.

Accidents caused by a stall began to litter the airwaves. Talk shows lit up with discussions concerning the sudden and rampant problem. People wanted answers, they wanted their elected officials to respond, and above all, they wanted to sue the oil companies. It was later discovered through attempted litigation that most governors had signed into legislation laws that prohibited individual citizens from suing an oil company or conglomerate. These companies were protected, they had rights that went far beyond the average citizen, and were shielded from angry consumers, local ordinances, and individual or class action lawsuits.

When prodded, the national government was content with giving the answer that they were hoarding gas for its war machine. It was too busy fighting other countries in trying to obtain their reserves or keeping shipping lanes open to bring the crude into their harbors, or guarding oil wells abroad from terrorists and other insurgents trying to cut civilizations off their supply lines of oil. The military was slowly becoming the world's police force, a police force for petroleum. It was a savage machine and required sacrifices from everyone, especially its citizens back home.

Clive was a government operative whose sole purpose was to help sway public opinion. The use of such tactical operations were designed to deceive the public, tricking it into thinking a foreign group or radicalized domestic organization was behind the effort. In the case of their petroleum ruse, he was there to influence a nation into going in a much more conservative direction with its use, and if it all played out the way they wanted, the government would begin to introduce rationing in the coming years.

When he first got his assignment, the task seemed simple enough. They had given him five subjects in which to antagonize. He was to stall at least one of their vehicles on the tracks of an approaching train. The accident that followed would make national headlines, bringing attention to the pleas from the government for the public to turn in their gas guzzling modes of transportation.

Clive would spend the next few weeks narrowing down his selection of potential victims, charting their routines compared to the information made available to him in the reports. He only needed one victim, one he felt would garner enough attention through the news media after the accident had occurred. He remembered why he finally decided on Salma Taupe. The single female was regimented in her scheduling, rarely, if ever, late to work. She had a routine on her time off of doing laundry, working out, and cleaning her apartment. She worked long hours but still struggled to make ends meet, and because of her schedule had no real time to meet anyone, let alone date, so she was free of any real commitments like a family. Selma was the perfect example of an individual that had become disenchanted with life, overwhelmed in the garbage heap of society's ills, but was still going through the daily grind because it was the only way she knew how to survive. Everyone out there could relate, and so that made her target one.

He noticed that on her way to and from work she crossed a set of busy train tracks, and that her evening commute was perfectly timed with a commuter train on those same rails. He found a wooded observation point on top of a small hill that overlooked the entire event. He would be able to remain undetected as he staged the operation from that vantage point.

Her silver Bronco would make quite an impression on the news and in the paper after it had been smashed to pieces by the train. If she bailed at the last second and survived that was alright by Clive. She didn't necessarily need to perish in this accident, and in fact, if she were still alive to give some interviews and confirm her vehicle had actually stalled on the tracks, it was all the better for those pulling the strings.

He leaned forward in his chair and reached for the bourbon. Grisly memories haunting him now, and if he wasn't cautious of them, they would intertwine and pry him apart. He was feeling a tremendous amount of guilt for pushing the button on that control pad, and all he wanted to do was whitewash his mind of everything that happened after it. He snapped the band around the neck of the bottle and twisted the cap off. The potent smell of alcohol caught him off guard, it smelled more like an isopropyl, and he thought, for an instant, he had bought the wrong bottle of booze. Checking the label confirmed what he had purchased from the state store and he took another sniff, only this time he caught the faint oaky scent that was promised.. He slowly poured the contents in a glass. The caramelized coloring made him feel as if he were about to indulge in a part something special from his father's generation. He set the bottle down and with one arm brought the glass against his chest. Rocking back and forth he could clearly see the images of the accident flashing through his mind.

He sat on the hill of the wooded observation point and watched as her Bronco approached, holding the square trigger device in his hands, the antenna extended toward her truck, waiting for it to get closer to the tracks. The timing of everything was working brilliantly. He could see the commuter train off in the distance as it wound its way hugging the river. Eventually, the engine and its cars would break off and head toward the station located in this part of town. The difference between the two traveling entities was about ten minutes apart, and he felt really good for how it was all setting up.

The rail crossing guards were still in their upright positions as Salma approached the tracks. Clive glanced at the box he was holding to make sure the small green light was still flashing to reflect signal strength. He allowed his thumb to float over the large red button he was to push to cause her vehicle to stall. He watched as the Bronco approached and just at the right time felt his thumb flex in response, and as he pushed the button her vehicle glided to a halt, sitting dead square in the middle of the tracks.

Clive could hear her trying to restart it and began pulling for her to exit the stalled vehicle.

"C'mon Salma, think about where you are at. Give up on it. Get out of that damn truck."

The train was just coming into view with its bright headlight on, flickering slightly as it hit the uneven joints of the track, the horn began to blow—the engineer was well aware of the Bronco in front of him.

He looked back to the Bronco. The woman was struggling inside. At first Clive thought she was caught up in her seatbelt, but she had worked her way to the backseat.

"What the hell are you doing? Get out of the goddamn truck lady!"

The train closed in with its horn blaring and its wheels locking—the engineer frantically trying to stop.

Within the Bronco suddenly a child's face pressed up against the glass. Clive felt his gut seize up, and the panic robbed him of his breath. At this distance with everything happening, she would have never heard him, but he still wished he could have screamed out to her, to tell her to get out of the Bronco. Salma was frantically trying to release the passenger side door. The child's face was panicked and frightened as the train bared down on them. Salma kept trying desperately to get the door open but never succeeded.

The sickening screech of twisted metal brought a wave of nausea to Clive as he watched the train decimate the vehicle, pushing it the down the tracks until it broke apart like a paper toy. The train's horn blared the entire time until the engine stopped well beyond the crossing.

Clive scanned the debris field hoping to spot some sign one of them had made it, that they had been thrown clear of the relentless push of the train. After a few minutes a sizeable fire broke out in the remains of the Bronco, people exited the train trying to do something about it, but he already knew it was too late and that no one within that Bronco had survived.

He grabbed the glass of bourbon with the same hand he had held the controller in, shaking a bit, he quite unexpectedly tossed the drink back as if it were a shot. The sting was as shockingly bitter as its initial scent, and he bit all the way to the sides of his face compacting his cheeks in a forced grimace. Drinking it, shooting it, nothing he did tarnished the image he had in his head of that child in the backseat with his small hands pressing against the window, his confused panicked look driving home the fact he wasn't going to make it. He was never given the chance.

Clive had a difficult time complaining about anything after that. There really wasn't a point to griping about not getting a fair shake, it was absurd. He had taken that option off the table for Salma and her nephew. Her sister had dropped the child off as Selma was getting ready to leave work, so she and her husband could go out for the evening. Now, in the aftermath there was nothing Clive could do to assuage the situation, for he lacked the strength to settle any of the issues he had buried deep within. He would find drinking far easier in aiding his attempts at self-therapy, and there were days when he drank that he tried to find the strength within himself to pick up his pistol and end his sorrow, but he couldn't even pull that off. Just like he couldn't find the courage to look at himself in the mirror on the days he felt guilty, and those days were quite often. He began to forget what he looked like and wanted it to stay that way, he wanted to be invisible. It was a stretch and something he would never be able to maintain, much in the same vein of when he told himself he was still a good guy.

CHAPTER THREE – OF TOKAMAKS AND MIGHTY OAKS

Tindra was the well-kept secret that two students might exchange information about in the tunnels connecting the dorms and classrooms on the campus of MIT. Most, if not all, of her work, was obtained by word of mouth, on the slow breath of a whisper and usually backed up with a scrap of paper containing her number scrawled across it to a student needing help. Plenty of semesters had passed since she arrived, moving past the crassness of Nicolas Prin and to a new set of goal-oriented students. The work she had contracted out over the years at the university seemed innocent enough, organizing and typing out research notes, transcribing lectures, or the writing of a lengthy term paper, but even then most of her clients had done their homework, they really did just need her typing skills to finish the job.

Still, she had a difficult time believing she was a line item on any student's budget back at their parent's manor. Her clients may have come from well-to-do families, and those families most certainly were unwittingly paying her, but no one really needed to know. Just like the students that used those tunnels to get from one class to another, the information and knowledge about Tindra tended to stay underground, and that's the way she liked it.

The origins of hacking were like that as well, staying completely out of sight, but had a totally different context as to what one would normally think the term would currently apply. MIT became immersed in this concept, its long rich history speckled with legendary tales of thoroughly thought out practical jokes. The great hacks demonstrated expert planning, supreme originality, all the while showing an appreciation for what they were lampooning. For instance, they placed a replica of a campus police car on top of the Great Dome, no easy feat, but those sent to investigate the matter found the police car to include a mannequin dressed as an officer holding a cup of coffee with a box of donuts placed in the passenger seat. There was the time hackers built a wall and disguised it as a bulletin board, covering the entrance of the newly arriving president's office. The university at that time was putting up new boards within buildings around campus, so this fit right in with the theme of the semester. The incoming president wandered the halls looking for his office until it was finally figured out. The prank itself received national headlines. It is even rumored that once an MIT student snuck out onto the Harvard football field to feed the pigeons, he blew a referee whistle before he threw the seed, conditioning the birds to fly onto the field to look for the food. At the start of the football season, just before the Harvard players took the field, the referee blew his whistle and hordes of pigeons stormed the gridiron in search of lunch.

The hacks at MIT were never meant to hurt anyone, this was part of the hacker's code, cruelty was seen as being too easy, unimaginative, and careless.

When the act of hacking first landed in the world of computing it was in the confines of computer labs and was initially looked at as a tool for picking apart a function, for circumventing a system, finding an unchecked backdoor to a program, a hiccup that could be exploited, or weaknesses in the coding itself. The method for breaking things down in this manner was used to show existing problems or limitations with a particular program to those who designed them. It wasn't long before a new set of individuals outside of the bounds of universities began to look at these glaring gaps as another way they could extend their own capabilities and leverage these programs for their own means.

This marked the beginning to a kind of lawlessness humanity had only ever seen at the edges of a frontier, with unchecked, wide-open spaces, individuals saying or doing whatever they wanted whenever they wanted, and with plenty of ways to hide. By the time law enforcement began to take cybercrimes seriously, a new deeper more mysterious layer had emerged to evade them, the creation of the Dark Web. There were those individuals using the internet who saw it as being too transparent, too open. They had ideas that were counter to society, counter to any law-abiding citizen, and counter, of course, to what the web was really supposed to be about, which was an open platform for knowledge.

There were nefarious activities associated with this deeper layer of the web, most of which Tindra found completely abhorrent. It sickened her to know child molesters, hitmen, and content as frightening as snuff films existed within these peer-to-peer networks. They had to, no one in their right mind would ever own up to doing these things, let alone house them on a central server asking to be discovered and reported on. One needed to obtain specific software and authorization codes to access any of the content on the dark web, and once there, were sent directly to a person's computer or mainframe. Nothing about the Dark Web would have interested her if it weren't for two things, one was the fact that this was where computer hackers offered up their services, and for Tindra hacking was the natural next step in evolving her typing capabilities. Eventually, she was able to link up with a hacking group to form a loose-knit partnership. The other reason to be on the dark web was payment, a form of digital currency was used to complete transactions, and this was how hackers and other people on the Dark Web got reimbursed.

Tindra's introduction to coding came out of the desperation of one engineering student trying to complete his project on time, when this team leader got her name he was told she was an exceptional typist who wrote research and term papers. He knew it was a stretch to have her help on his project in the Plasma Science and Fusion Center but went ahead and asked for her number anyway. What he was really looking for was someone to write the more redundant code for his experiment on the design and performance of current Drive Systems in the ion cyclotron range of frequencies or the ICRF, and wave dampening.

It was rumored that the funding would soon be running out as the government was trimming down its budget for these types of experimental fusion reactors. A Tokamak was a large donut shaped device that had plasma racing through the inner core, while powerful magnets lined the outside of the device and were there to keep the plasma moving. If a bank of magnets failed the plasma would adhere to the side of the wall where the failure took place, the damage was so severe in most instances, it would take almost a year to clean up and repair the mess. Magnets failed all the time in Tokamaks, with some of the best running times lasting a little over a minute. This may have seemed like a lot of work for very little functionality, but the first to harness this technology would literally be sitting on an unlimited power source that was also very clean, so it was difficult to understand why the government would turn their back on this potential, but it should have come as no surprise, this wasn't the first time the government walked away from helping its citizens attain a better way of life.

MIT had a few nuclear reactors come and go on its site, with the first one constructed in 1958, the 6 megawatt reactor was built solely for research purposes. Getting the Nuclear Regulatory Commission to approve another test facility on its site was no small feat, but the chance of obtaining unlimited power was too tempting of a deal to pass on, and so the Alcator was greenlit, assembled back in 1973 the Alcator A was coming up on its first revision and moving toward Alcator B, but they couldn't generate enough power for the upgrade and when the funding finally got approved for the revision it was quickly moved past the 'B' phase and toward Alcator C. This Tokamak reactor functioned experimentally until the mid-eighties, then a so-called modification was done because the budget was turned down for Alcator D. Using the power supplies from Alcator C, a new Tokamak was assembled Alcator C Mod, with its construction getting approval in 1986.

Long since completed now, Alcator C Mod was ramping up to not only run tests on the IRCF but also a new type of fuel, this time trying helium-3 added to the deuterium and hydrogen mix. The student intern responsible for entering the coding into the computers on wave frequency and building the simulation was falling behind schedule, and this was how Tindra became called upon to help. Initially, he wanted her to type out a summary of the project, he felt that by her doing this he would get her up to speed on what they were trying to accomplish. Meanwhile, back in the lab, most of his student volunteers were finding the coding exasperating. They weren't inputting the data as fast as needed to meet his deadline, and he didn't want to be the one responsible for postponing their schedule. Watching Tindra type, it soon became apparent to the team leader that he was wasting an extremely useful resource, and she soon found herself in front of one of the computers dedicated to the simulation.

For her, being placed in front of the monitor with its curser flashing, waiting for her to type in a command, was intimidating, for some silly reason. There weren't any fancy icons prompting her to do something, no browser she could comb through and research a question she may have had, this was straight-up raw computing power that only offered a blank screen as a portal to get in. Her fingers felt frozen as she took in the concept for this kind of data entry, hoping to find a point in which to anchor from. The team leader leaned over her shoulder and began to instruct her on what to do, how the computer would respond to the code she was typing in, and how to check it for errors once she was finished writing her lines. She began hitting the keys just like the other students seated in that room, at their same moderate pace, but after a few hours, this would soon change. It may have been true that she didn't know a thing about computer programming, but she took to this new challenge as if it were a long-lost language that needed to be cracked. Once she began to understand its basics, she devoured what it had to offer until she became fluent in its use. Tindra would also gain a reputation for being relentless in her efforts for solving things, with her fingers flying across the keyboard knocking out task after task, coding got done, programs functioned, and because of it, the limitless world of cyberspace began revealing itself to her.

The one thing that became very apparent early on in her travels within the vast electronic landscape of the internet was retrieving the truth, pure, unaltered truth. Someone always had a take on a fact, a spin on what was being reported and couldn't help their bias when retelling it. Others got so wound up by a story that may not agree with their sensibilities that they felt there had to be more to it, underlying circumstances that were waiting to be unearthed. If the facts didn't fit their paradigm, they would usually accuse those who were in charge of staging a cover-up.

Tindra found the internet was the one medium that allowed disjointed thoughts to flourish, and because of people's constant use and belief in it, society soon followed in its footsteps, losing patience when things didn't move fast enough, or their attention when there wasn't enough excitement. Much like a virus, the more contact someone had with it, the more likely a person was to be infected. Instead of people becoming socially conscious, they became ultrasensitive to their social media status. Instead of pushing to become more active in the physical world, they pushed to get in touch with a virtual one. Instead of seeking to become astutely civic-minded, they embraced a lawlessness driven by lines of code. They settled for fake friends, followed outlandish rumors, and allowed themselves to be influenced by the opinions of those who spent their entire day trolling. In her opinion, people were becoming reactive instead of proactive. She found people thinking like this all around her and tough to combat, but she pushed back and fought in the same way every voter is left to decipher the truth for themselves.

It was a world that was upside down, where the judiciary would hold no one liable, and allow for politicians to outright lie. The chaos the world was facing started within this country. With no one being held accountable in politics, prejudice reared its ugly head, and politicians went after their opponents, undermine law enforcement, and rebut and stonewall any checks and balances that questioned their ultimate authority. It was a system that allowed those seeking total control and power to thrive. Campaigns of hate and misinformation bombarded the average citizen, it was taken as standard fair. The Environmental, Food and Drug, and Agricultural Agencies were made to look foolish. They were accused of consciously lying to the public, of wasting tax payer's dollars, and were too controlling of the average citizen in their oversight. Those looking to sweep aside these agencies would say anything to break them apart and weaken their influence.

Tindra swam through all of it, trying to keep her head above the waterline, not to be held under and drown in the tidal wave of bullshit coming from the top. She kept waiting, hoping for the day someone would finally take a system they said was broken and fix it, to bring it back to the level it once was created for in helping people in need, but no one ever came forward and fixed it. Having clarity in government meant the people had a voice and she began to wonder if letting it stay broke was the point of those elected officials keeping their power.

THE STATE OF THE STATE

The air was literally abuzz, filled with various full-sized drones, bug-sized spies, or platforms of sensitive listening gear housed in jet aircraft flying high overhead. It was all up there, the whole apparatus, hovering constantly making the country safe from the threat of extremists, or so they said. There were those in society who weren't buying it, who were opposed to this type of surveillance, who were against the spread of it and its inevitable lead into wiretapping and the combing of phone records. It was an unwanted intrusion into their personal space. Tindra had heard the arguments against such domestic reconnaissance, but some of those individuals were unrealistic in their wishes, wanting to go back to a time when the biggest piece of technology a person could own was a color television set, and their telephones were still slaved to a rotary.

She wasn't buying into that line of thought, once people got a taste for technology it grew on them, became a part of who they were, they developed an appetite for it, and fought hard to attain and keep it. There was no way they were ever going to be able to put the genie back in the bottle, now that was a truth.

Tindra had done her fair share of combing the internet looking for facts and they were difficult to come by but hidden in the saturated layers of misinformation was always a kernel of it. She found even lies needed a hint of truth to survive. If a lie grew it's because they found fertile ground in fear and ignorance, like mushrooms kept in the dark they grew best in a bed of shit. The drones and surveillance craft high up above had a part in creating this gigantic bag of manure everyone seemed to find themselves trapped in. However, she couldn't imagine a person monitoring every single one of these devices, some of this collected content had to be falling through the cracks. It followed then, she thought they had no good reason for monitoring her, especially with the large mounds of dung continuously forming all around her.

Occasionally Tindra searched the web for inspiration, it may have been a feel-good story, a self-help talk, or something as simple as a quote. It was in this vein she stumbled across a quote which foreshadowed things to come: *a person's self portrait of insignificance is only allowed to endure for as long as one walks in their sleep.*

It read more like a riddle than a line meant to bestow inspiration, but when she would look back on it some years later this was the precursor to her awakening. Tindra's wakeup call came on the heels of a news story, a news story that seemed so insignificant to her at the time that it's difficult to believe it would eventually submerge her in the deep end of Crypto-anarchism.

She read a report about the sarcophagus in the Ukraine failing, and how the international community was banding together to come up with a fix. The article was painting a dire picture of the slow collapse of this original structure having housed one of the worst nuclear accidents on the planet. She had heard of Chernobyl but didn't realize the magnitude of the damage the RBMK reactor had gone through. It spoke about the threat of radioactive dust that could get caught up into the atmosphere if the structure collapsed, and in her mind, it had to be one hell of a pile of dust being housed in that facility. She knew there had to be more to it than that and wanted to get a better picture of what was going on inside this crumbling cement shell.

Ordinarily an event like this would have never had her thinking twice about what was happening an entire continent away but working on the term project to heat plasma within a Tokamak reactor had her more in tune with the possible hazards nuclear power could deliver. She began combing the web for any type of news story that could fill her in on the extent of damage, but the Soviet Empire was very tight lipped on dolling that information out, it might have stemmed from political pride, but this lack of cooperation only fueled her curiosity to find out what they were hiding in that facility.

Searching for these facts had her plummeting deeper, diving well past the convenient portals of internet browsers, until she descended to the murky pools of the Dark Web. There she discovered a chatroom called Geiger Counter, it was established for the sharing and knowledge of mishaps and accidents in the nuclear field that were not being published in the mainstream.

The subject matter for this site wasn't just confined to civilian mismanagement, there was a whole list of military topics featured as well, with the headers for each reading like a list of failed nicknames for heavy weight boxers, there was Upshot-Knothole, Hardtack, Grenadier, and Mighty Oaks just to name a few. She clicked back to the civilian heading for nuclear accidents and was surprised to find so many to choose from, there were twenty-seven worldwide incidents to be exact, with Chernobyl being smack dab in the middle of them when listed in chronological order.

Initially it seemed people on the outside who were concerned about this accident had to piece it together through the use of publicly made photos from military satellites, radiation readings from neighboring countries, and intercepted communications that had been made public between the Kremlin and the nuclear plant at Pripyat. The Russian response to these accusations was immediate as they sent out messages asking for calm, downplaying the severity of the situation, and even claimed to be gaining control of the event. For them it was a matter of not wanting to look weak, of a dark state looking as if it were in control, but the limited amount of news stories she was able to come across spoke of an event completely out of control.

The first thing that got her attention were the reports of glowing graphite on the ground and lying on top of the remaining rooftops of building four itself. Some of the graphite was so hot it could be seen even in broad daylight. Any sign of used graphite outside of its containment chamber is an extreme hazard, period, end of story. Unfortunately for the rest of the world this wasn't the end of the story, but the terrible opening line to a frightful chapter in the nuclear almanac.

There were numerous accounts in the forum of high energy radioactive particles being released into the atmosphere. During the nights as the fires raged, and

43

for weeks afterward, a bright blue-white beam shot straight up into the air from the exposed core. This phosphorescence represented a release of atomic energy four-hundred times greater than the release of atomic energy at Hiroshima.

The files were extensive, with some feeling like firsthand accounts, they described in great detail on the night of the event that a test at the station to simulate a blackout was being run. The operators, young and inexperienced, erred on several checklist procedures, eventually scramming the reactor, or suddenly shutting it down. They did this by dumping cold water into the reactor and dropping the control rods. The rods were meant to absorb the reaction spurred on by the fuel and under normal circumstances that is exactly what would have happened. In this case though, the reactor was already in a very hot and unstable condition because of the mismanagement of the operators under instruction by their deputy chief engineer. The dumping of the cold water into the reactor had the opposite effect from what they desired, instead of cooling or slowing the heating taking place within, the dumping of water allowed for a rapid steam build up which caused tremendous pressure to build within the core and the plate at the top of the reactor to become dislodged, jamming the control rods in a halfway down position.

Researching graphite in reactors, she learned that it was used to regulate the uranium fuel rods. Graphite slows the firing of the isotopes, so they have a better chance at colliding, splitting, and releasing their energy.

The control rods were filled with boron and the further they were placed into the reactor, the more they were able to absorb the reaction happening inside the core.

The stuck control rods with their graphite tips were actually having an opposite effect inside the reactor, helping to accelerate the colliding and splitting of isotopes, creating a tremendous amount of heat. The operators at Chernobyl seeing that the control rods were stuck again dumped water into the spiking reactor in an attempt to cool it down. The cold water caused fuel fragmentation and a deadly buildup of steam. It exploded, blowing the lid off the reactor and the building apart. Graphite, fuel, and tons of other radioactive debris showered the site.

The international community soon detected the deadly dust moving with the wind. A radioactive cloud so potent that a downwind forest turned blood red. Only when the international community revealed what was happening within Chernobyl did the Russian leaders ordered the evacuation of Pripyat— a full thirty-six hours after the accident. During this time, the people were directly exposed to the radioactive ash venting from the exposed core.

Tindra came across the story about the three divers who volunteered to go into the water and open a drain valve. The floors beneath the damaged reactor were filled with the water that was meant for the core. Since it was damaged, and could not retain the water meant for it, the water moved to the lower levels as the site was now transitioning into a meltdown phase. Radioactive molten lava was heading for this stagnant pool of water, and if it reached it would cause an even more massive steam build up and explosion, releasing enough radiation to threaten the entire continent. The three divers swam into these flooded radioactive areas, opened the hatches by hand, and released the water and averted the threat.

She read in horror the decisions they made in using army personnel in areas where cleaning robots could not reach, which was up on the rooftops of building four, and other difficult areas where radioactive debris had been thrown. The men cleared these areas of the graphite and other materials, throwing it back into the destroyed building. Those men had to hustle, keep running once in a cleanup zone, because the levels of radiation were so deadly any one soldier could not spend more than ninety seconds at a time on that roof.

This enormous tragedy was what they had covered up in the cement of the Sarcophagus, all the graphite, the melted core, and the destroyed building itself. This was why the international community was ringing the alarm bells again as this structure began to fall apart. There were people within the forum of this group demanding urgency in this matter. The tag for the chatroom relaying these warnings was direct enough; Chernobyl Heat.

It was headed by a moderator using the handle Lucifer1984 and he had several other conversation threads people were actively involved with. In those threads they talked about the possibility of Ukraine independence, the supposed ban of Russian citizens being allowed entry into this country, and several theories floated as to why the ambassadors really fled their embassy during the disaster at Chernobyl. Tindra read these with interest and monitored the live chats without ever really participating. To her these threads became the word on the street, the back story of what was really going on, it was an information dump that had escaped the mainstream. It got her riled up and wanting to know more, wanting to know how the moderators of this site were able to get information no one else seemed to be talking about. Her desire for more knowledge would lead her down a rabbit hole that would continually splinter off and keep going, seemingly to never end, and it would all start with an unexpected request.

While reading an active conversation in one of the chatrooms, she was suddenly caught off guard by a message that was written directly to her. The requestor was none other than Lucifer1984, and he was asking her to make herself available the following day in a different chatroom known as the Gator Pool.

Users knew of the Gator Pool; it was a secure chatroom rarely anyone got invited to. And if people had experienced what went on in there, they weren't sharing it online. She sat there staring at the screen knowing full well they had been monitoring her at the computer science lab at MIT. The screen became an ominous object; it was creeping into her life without ever leaving the desk. She knew it to be unblinking and unfeeling; it was like staring into a deep dark well, hoping, at some point, she would see the bottom. The problem of being on a peer-to-peer network; one was able to look at the files on another person's computer just as they were able to view the one using it. Her vulnerability in this scenario began to unfold until she had the inclination to jump out of her chair and yank the internet cable out of the wall. She would have done it to if she wasn't seated with other students working on their projects in that computer lab. Lucifer1984 certainly knew where she was doing her internet snooping. The request hovered on the screen until, hands shaking, she confirmed it. She then received their log-in information, and after that, the screen went dark.

The blinking cursor was the only clue that the computer was still up and running.

MIGHTY OAKS

The horizontal tunnel known as U12t ran under the Rainer Mesa in the Southern portion of the Nevada Nuclear Test Site. Horizontal testing had been going on for well over a decade, so in planning, there was little concern over the methodology or how they would contain the blast of the small nuclear device they had placed inside. Most testing was being done to determine potentials for new weapon systems that would eventually become the MX Missile, improvements on individual Multiple Re-entry Warheads, or as of late, space-based weapons for the newly proposed Star Wars defense system.

Channel Krier was approaching the tunnel entrance with three other individuals in tow. They were supposed to be there on standby as part of the emergency response team in case something went wrong with the test, and as it happened something did. Channel was one of two people holding a Geiger Counter, taking readings as they approached the entrance, listening to the device tick rapidly as if a baseball card were being struck by the rotating spokes of a moving bicycle. This was usually the type of Geiger Counter action that prompted most people who heard it to drop what they were doing and run. However, Channel knew the dosages they could get away with dressed in their cumbersome radioactive suits, they weren't quite pushing that barrier yet, the millisieverts weren't registering high enough.

The entrance to the tunnel was simmering, it was crazy to think of the earth as being baked, but it was, with thick wafts of white smoke dancing from the shaft. He was less than a hundred yards away from the entrance, getting closer with each step, and his Geiger Counter was ticking away now giving him the occasional high pitched feedback.

The initial reports said a few of the safety hatches had failed to close during the blast. The horizontal tunnel had two parts to it, one was the long corridor that was considered the entrance, the second part of the tunnel was an even longer corridor that was considered the test chamber. The testing equipment contained within the long tunnel were as close to the entrance as possible to make it easy under normal circumstances, to retrieve the test results without having to spend more time than needed in the radioactive compartment.

Far underground at the center of the mesa was the hollowed-out chamber where the small nuclear device was detonated. The chamber was designed, in part, as a containment vessel, harnessing most of the energy from the explosion. It was for a brief moment that this energy was allowed out of the chamber and into the long tunnel, where the testing gear was located.

There were no reports of long flames ferociously licking the ground in front of the entrance to the cave by the observers but seeing the charred marks on the ground suggested otherwise. There was some billowing smoke pouring out of the entrance during the test, not enough to suggest the secured doors hadn't done their part in sealing off the main chamber, but how could he know, he hadn't ever been part of a failed attempt. As per procedures, the entrance doors were remotely opened now so that Channel and his team members could approach and get a good look inside, and so he suspected this was the reason now for the smoke that was in the air. They would remain open until they retrieved the data, to include their Geiger Counter readings, and then would be sealed up again.

His legs were heavy as he walked toward the cave entrance, with each step his legs felt as if they were gaining weight. He was breathing with difficulty into his radiation mask, its filters stuck out like circular gills attached to his cheeks and blocked large amounts of air from escaping. It was more work than expected to expel the carbon dioxide. His mask filled with the mist and heat of his exhale, making it difficult to see until the next intake of oxygen. The air in the tanks they wore was cooler than the air outside which helped with defogging his mask, but that wouldn't last long as the heat from the Nevada Desert began to cook the contents of those tanks.

That wasn't the only thing cooking out here, if those inner chamber doors didn't close during the blast there was no telling how much of the testing gear would survive. Losing that gear would be something those in charge would frown upon, but that was nothing in comparison to the uncontrolled venting that was now taking place. Seeing the white smoke that began to waft out into the air in greater and greater plumes from the cave, he knew all too well this had to be true, and perhaps one of the doors did not close as it should have. There would be hell to pay for this if there had been an uncontrolled release of radiation.

They were instructed as a general rule once the Geiger Counter began to sing at a level that eliminated any clicking they would have to immediately turn back. It was difficult to get someone with a knowledge of nuclear physics to advance any further listening to that loud whiny sound. A reading like that would shower several lifetime's worth of radiation down upon them.

Channel looked up into the clear blue sky and wondered which way the prevailing winds were blowing. If they were coming out of the northwest, like they were known to do, states East of the Rockies would be receiving a dusting from this accident. There weren't enough suits or bomb shelters in the country for every person to get into, and he had no idea how they were going to explain themselves once the regulators out in the field began to report radioactive readings.

When the device was detonated in its chamber the doors down this corridor were to remain open only for a fraction of a second, allowing just enough gamma radiation out to test the viability of designing a weapon in space using this technique. The proposal spoke of having sentinels of these space-based weapons at the ready, a theoretical line in the sand which no one could cross, forget about warheads, this would be a beam of concentrated radiation raining down out of the sky, a wall of intense electromagnetic waves knocking out everything tied to any type of electronic equipment, making those things inoperative. The experiment's unofficial nickname was Mighty Oak, taken from one of Aesop's Fables titled; The Oak and the Reed. One of the lines from the fable read; "A reed before the wind lives on, while mighty oaks do fall, tis better to bend than break." In this case, the wind was the massive electromagnetic pulse that would be generated from their futuristic hypothetical weapon.

There was something immediate to consider as they investigated, related to what happened under the Rainer Mesa, where they would discover that the failure of a door closure happened in the testing corridor because a chisel had been placed on the floor between the lead door and frame.

They didn't want to call it sabotage, but it was difficult to see how it could be anything but, and much like the venting of radiation into the atmosphere from the failure of this test, there would be little reporting of this intentional disruption to anyone on the outside.

CHAPTER FOUR – THE AMBUSH

He dropped a large cube into the glass and poured himself another drink.

Clive Vanderjack wasn't the same agent they had recruited all those years ago, and he wasn't trying to be. Back then, he was the trusted soldier who was recognized by his battalion commanders for his ability to follow orders, engage an enemy, and always make it back to their designated rendezvous point. Neither rain, nor sand, nor lack of sleep kept him from achieving his goals, and the government realized his talents were being wasted on a conflict they were not playing to win. He was brought back to the states after only one tour of duty to be trained as a social provocateur.

Now, he could no longer identify with the agent they had trained and sent out on assignments to disrupt the fiber of society. That duty was now falling to younger agents, and there should have been no surprise on his part because it always fell to the younger agents, they were the ones who were still excited about their jobs. Those were the candidates they continually molded and endlessly tested. Their loyalties were being questioned each day they were out in the field, and that was whether they knew it or not. The agency was looking for the weak, or those that had fallen in with a fifth column. Performing to the expectations of their superiors was the only way they would survive within the agency. At some point within Clive's career, things changed, and he was no longer in line for coveted assignments, he became the heavy, the blunt instrument used to send a message to an individual or an organization. No longer did he feel a part of the team, the national push by those in charge of guiding the population into a New World Order.

He might have felt bad about his subtle unannounced reassignment if it hadn't been for the fact that the administration had already, by and large, succeeded in their goals by the time they were passing him over, mission accomplished. They had planted so much doubt within the people about the legitimacy of the press, of local and national elections, and of who our allies and enemies were supposed to be. No one had time to delve into these issues because everyone was clamoring for a job and in most areas of the country being employed was a big deal. Those who landed a job felt fortunate, appreciated whatever wage was offered them, and as part of their deal memo could not complain about their working conditions no matter how unsafe. Local governments swayed in the same type of breeze, politicians were free to rob their coffers, bankrupting them, which in turn destroyed the infrastructure of that neighborhood. The national government's fix, or response to this was to enact a type of martial law claiming it was the only way to save those localized broken political systems.

As time passed, people got used to dealing with things like war rationing, martial law, and with no real legal way to protest. This was the way of the world, not that any of it mattered to Clive, their rules didn't apply to him. Being a government agent had its perks, had him placed above such oppressive sanctions, and that was because every agent needed to have the ability to see and move above the fray, have the feeling of being able to breathe on their own, and to make the correct decisions in keeping the population in check. All he ever had to do was flash his badge at the grocery store and he was shown the special produce room that hadn't been picked through by the normal hordes of customers, was able to obtain clothing at the department store that wasn't second hand and actually fit him, or lived in a gated neighborhood that was usually reserved for the well-to-do. His badge allowed him to pass through check points or ride the shoulder of a highway to get around a traffic delay. The local authorities didn't want him around, so they never had a problem waving him through or telling him to be on his way.

Being on his way, that was the soothing, serene thought that finally snapped him out of his dismal funk. He had been sitting on the couch for the past hour staring at a blank wall. He got up on occasion to grab an ice cube and freshen his drink. He closed his eyes and rubbed them roughly until he felt he had squeezed the last remaining tears from his ducts. He looked down at his worn, thin cushions to see the folders, photos, and bound reports spread out over the coarse fabric. The work scattered across his couch had come to represent almost two years of persistent surveillance, some contained reports by outside consultants who had combed through the data, as well as poignant opinions by experts from within the department, and the ruling of the oversight committee who had final say in the case the surveillance team was looking to build.

Within the pages were the detailed descriptions of individuals who spent most of their time hacking into computers, disrupting communication links by flooding call centers, canceling legitimate bank or credit card accounts of other people, or opening dummy accounts within a business unaware of their iniquitous activity. From the looks of some of their hacks, they had even gotten their hands on a few of the test sets telephone lineman would use. Phone lines still existed, crisscrossing the country, and were one of the few ways a small town could access the internet. The people who started hacking into the phone lines in the early sixties referred to it as *phreaking,* it was about experimenting and exploring the phone network, and in the end, to suss out what systems were connected to it.

The group under investigation became so emboldened that they started placing phone calls to companies fishing for information that would help them in their hacks, or getting the person answering the phone to unwittingly turn on a mainframe or hard drive that was housed in the building so the group could begin hacking and try to gain access to the information contained within.

It was difficult at first to see the real harm in these acts, with law enforcement initially not planning on taking any action viewing most of what they had done as exaggerated pranks, but as the hacking group honed their skills they began to radically exploit and reroute the telephone system. This interference with the inner workings of the phone company was what raised the red flags and started the investigation to find out what their real intent might be.

The internet had been around as a defense department network and also served as an experimental laboratory for the computer sciences as early as the 1960's. This fact surprised Clive because he hadn't heard anything about the medium until a few browser companies started to advertise themselves as an internet provider in the early eighties. As he got older he shied away from using such technology, for he saw nothing good ever coming from entering one's personal information onto such sites, not that his opinion mattered much, but he knew there were technicians back at the Maryland Procurement Office who had been monitoring the people using these services, even back then, watching as they bonded through their use of chatrooms and fledgling social-media platforms.

The use of chatrooms seemed odd to Clive because of the slow pacing of the conversations compared to when one used a phone or spoke in person, but there was something that enticed a younger generation to use it, and that was probably because the internet was free, away from the prying eyes of parents, or the control of employers, or as most poorly assumed, the government. Clive had a hard time believing the technology for this would keep someone glued to their computer screen for hours on end, but he was obviously way off base on this hunch because the four individuals singled out in these reports for abusing this technology were in front of their computers for an inordinate amount of time. They operated under pseudonyms, or what was more commonly referred to in the computer world as a *user name*. Commandant2600, Lucifer1984, Ideologue5150, and Enigma9000 were the four primary case folders given to Clive, sure there were others that came and went in their group, but these were the four main players. Clive was to put a team together of his own choosing with the sole purpose of setting these hackers up so they then could be arrested. Once in the legal system, their past crimes could be brought out into the light, they would be exposed for the law breakers they were, and then justice would be served.

Persona Non Grata was a computer activist group who got its name because some of its users were banned from time to time from an early chatroom called *Civic Struggle,* the site specialized in whistleblowing and pointing out the political discord that racked both parties. The conversations within the forums were promoted as being serious in nature, they wanted true debate, and frowned upon reckless postings or what would become known as trolling. If things got too carried away along these lines the moderator stepped in and would erase the post and lock the user out for a period of time, giving them the tagline Persona Non Grata in place of the user's name.

It was out of spite that users like Commandant2600 and Lucifer1984 went back to the site once the ban on their names was lifted and torched the forums with political rhetoric, name calling, and factious topics meant for hyperbole rather than debate. After repeatedly being blocked by the moderator they were eventually banned from the site altogether.

This caused one of the others in the group, identified as Ideologue5150, to pose as a representative from the site in a phone call to the hosting company, there she obtained the user name and password for one of the admins. Ideologue5150 and the others then hacked into Civic Struggle and changed the homepage so that only the words Persona Non Grata showed up on the main screen. To add insult to injury, the group also launched a Denial of Service attack, which meant they flooded the server with so many requests that the real users were essentially locked out for over a week. Anyone wanting to participate on Civic Struggle during that time was stuck looking at a home page announcing their overall ban.

Civic Struggle became the group's first official act of electronic disobedience, there was more to come as the group now felt it had a purpose, and that purpose was to police the internet of injustice, or call out injustice as it occurred in society, and then posting their grievances on line. Very few times in any of the reports did Persona Non Grata ever single out an individual, it was usually a group or organization, some entity that was flexing its muscle in an unfair way toward the public, or perhaps weren't acting on the behalf of the public when it should have been.

They targeted everything from Fortune 500 Companies, school systems, banks, and even law enforcement. Nothing was above reproach, and by all reports they were becoming more and more emboldened with who they were calling out and attacking, and that was because they were gaining more and more of a following. It was surprising how many people, especially young people, were supporting what Persona Non Grata came to represent. The internet had become a place where people could freely protest at any time and talk about anything. In the eyes of the government however, the group had gone rogue in this electronic medium.

There was one file Clive had in his possession that contained nothing but photos from demonstrations Persona Non Grata participated in, lots of photos of people in attendance and all wearing the same shoddy mask. The movie *Shrill* came out a few years back in which the antagonist tormented his victims wearing a theater mask whose upper features around the eyes and forehead took on the texture of a doily but were exaggerated in such a way that the waffled-out holes looked frightening. The masks weren't a big seller, likely because the movie wasn't as big of a hit with fans as certain costume shops had hoped, and so there were plenty of masks left over after the Halloween season that following year. This simple disguise was cheap and the group adopted the look immediately with people buying the mask year-round for their Persona Non Grata public gatherings, and as the group's popularity kept rising, more and more shops kept the masks in stock.

Those files contained photos that were hand marked with red circles around suspected individuals they felt represented the four people of interest. Each of them in the photos was adorned with their own scarves, bandannas, hats, gloves, or hooded sweatshirts that kept most, if not all of their body, from being exposed. Still, the masks didn't cover their faces completely and there were indications as to who they might be judging from things like their five o'clock shadows, beards, or in some instances, lipstick. Tying this in with their body size, favorite articles of clothing, subsequent colors and styles, the shoes they wore, all of it went towards helping the investigators denote who might be who, and of course their gender, which for some reason surprised Clive that a woman would be mixed up in this.

With Persona Non Grata's extensive computer knowledge there were growing concerns about what future moves the group might take to make a statement, how they could use their powers to influence the general public, with some officials becoming fearful the group would begin targeting elections and challenging those in power.

Attacking the elections didn't make sense to Clive, not with how many voter restrictions they had in place. The fights were tough, the opposition didn't go down easily but gains were made in pulling most of the voting polls from poorer neighborhoods where the threat of fraud was prevalent. The creation of central voting hubs got the message across to everyone that if one wanted to cast a vote one would need to travel far and wait. These voting hubs were easier to monitor by officials and were outfitted with extensive identification equipment to make sure the intended voter was who they said they were and in complete compliance with the voting laws. Some complained that the oversight was intimidating, while others argued that the intimidation worked. There was no indication from any of the data to say Persona Non Grata planned to impact an election from beyond the shadows, but it was the threat of it just like voter fraud.

The seeds for these concerns probably wove their way into the halls of a congressional sub-committee on national surveillance. There wasn't a paper trail leading him to think this way, but Clive had been around the agency long enough to know how it all worked. Someone within those chambers felt threatened, they weren't able to sway a majority to take up legal action, and so in the privacy of their own office, or in the dark corner of one of the halls, they had a conversation on how to drum up a solution to this domestic problem. The only thing usually left to hash out after such a meeting was to what degree the response should be.

IDEOLOGUE5150

Clive had poured over these files time and again, but for some reason kept coming back to the dossier of Ideologue5150. It wasn't because he viewed this person as anymore of a threat than the others, or that he thought the individual in question was the weakest link within the group. It was clear even in the report Ideologue5150 wasn't one to be exploited. Clive kept coming back to this file because he was shocked to find out that Ideologue5150 was the online persona of a very beautiful young woman.

Tindra was a person of interest in some of the largest hacks Persona Non Grata pulled off. Her skills in computing were considered first-rate, professional, which in the eyes of the state made her a danger, she was a dissonant plain and simple. By not putting her skill set to use out in the work force she was signaling to the state she wasn't doing anything productive. Despite the disapproval of her actions from those above him, Clive found himself trying to save her. He didn't know how to explain it and was sure his binge-drinking wasn't helping with how he was processing this information about her.

One of the ways he felt he was "helping" her was by picking a non-lethal method for striking at their group; there was a file in his possession which authorized him to use whatever force necessary in apprehending them. It was pretty standard, but this type of order often got abused by team leaders when bringing in a suspect or taking them down, no matter what the injury or its severity to those arrested the agents would often point to the file authorizing its use as their justification. In this case he was veering away from that folder, not even informing his team of its existence. They would go about it in a different way, by methodically going about setting them up by shutting down a substation which in turn would pull the plug on the power for the city. There was already a ton of information out there about how susceptible the electrical grid was to an attack. With all the experience his team had in these kind of operations, they could easily make it look as if Persona Non Grata were at the heart of such a disruption.

Turning out the lights on the entire city would surely garnish country-wide attention, but for some of those out there, it might paint Persona Non Grata in a favorable light. They might even be seen as heroes for accomplishing such a feat. There wasn't one person back at ops who wanted to see this group empowered by this stunt or be aided in their efforts to gather new recruits. This operation had to be executed in such a way that the public would recoil at the mere mention of their name. It was even suggested that multiple missions would have to be carried out in order to get the effect for what they were trying to accomplish.

There were plenty of programs that started as one-offs but were upgraded immediately once their full potential was realized in either swaying public opinion or radically controlling the population. For example, Chem-trails was a Gulf War plan that called for a one-time spraying of the armies in Iraq with an agent that caused memory problems, joint pain, respiratory disorders, and fatigue. It didn't take a genius to figure out that it's much easier to fight an army that has difficulty reacting to the mental challenges being thrown at it. The downside, of course, was the chemicals, or *soup,* used in covering these areas lasted a lot longer than anticipated and adversely effected the armies of the coalition when they were ordered to move into these sprayed areas.

Once the results of those medical reports started coming in on the soldiers who served in that first conflict, someone within the Maryland Procurement Office realized they were sitting on a possible solution for another problem the administration had been saddled with. Social Security programs were beginning to run out of money, the program suffered because of the goals and dreams by those of past generations desiring to have a healthier country. Each generation was living longer and longer into their retirement, and because of this healthier status, the funding for social security was running out, not to mention the pharmaceutical industry was taking a massive hit. *Operation Black Pepper* became the official unspoken name for the Chem-trail program and was done in an effort to advance the interests of big pharma. The government allowed for this because most of the other home-grown industries developed in the states had been exported overseas, one of the few lasting programs still standing within the country was the pharmaceutical industry.

In the past the government had bailed out plenty of businesses that needed their help, giving big banks breaks, divvied out long lasting contracts in support of aerospace and defense, and now the pharmaceutical industry had their hands out begging for a boost. That's when the planes started flying with their fuselages full of specialized soups to spray into the air and get the citizens to feel sick and ill again.

Clive would set aside time almost every day listening to the coded messages being broadcast on shortwave radio, they usually had a series of tones, pulses, or keywords that would repeat over and over again. In those repeating patterns were the lines of code informing him of what operations were in play for the week, and when they might happen. He would hook up a Vox Decoder to his shortwave radio and wait for it to give him the source numbers for that day. One could do it by ear if they really needed to, and whoever was attempting to do this came to appreciate the multiple number of times those messages were being repeated. To the average citizen, it would have been frightening to know the amount of information being conveyed through the use of this technology, but instead people were consumed by their cable television subscription, satellite dish reception, internet connection, gaming portal, or music downloads. These were all considered beautiful distractions to those operating within the world of the covert. It was the background noise to their background noise.

The knowledge gained from his shortwave radio afforded Clive opportunities to retreat into his home and not emerge until he discovered when they were finished spraying. He hunkered down while the wicked world played itself out, for days he would avoid the contaminated air, and during that time he was polluting his liver by drinking away his sorrows. There was little left for him to do, the world had gone mad, it was thick with plots for revenge, corruption, and setting people up. This was how big government flexed its muscle in business, they were the power brokers who were hungry for more, filling their coffers with the lump sums of the world's wealth, who went about settling old scores to make sure people knew they were always on the hook until the debt was paid, anything and everything justified their greed.

Clive didn't exactly enjoy playing the heavy in those scenarios, to be called upon as the muscle, it wasn't why he became an agent, but that didn't seem to matter to his employers. He was dirty now, with the filth of their dealings, he knew too much about how they did business, and if he said no to them now, it would have been taken as a sign of him not wanting to play ball anymore. It was a disrespect that wouldn't go unnoticed and in taking a turn like that meant he would have to go a long way in earning back their trust.

He never touched anyone directly, not like some he knew who would enter a residence and inflict a terror that left those victims bloodied and weeping for mercy, those were cries he never wanted to hear, and it was a style he never wanted to adopt. Instead, he went about studying the person, reading between the lines to find out what was important to them, what they had worked hard to achieve, and then he would burn it down or damage it enough to get the point across. The message for that kind of vandalism usually got their attention, and if it didn't wake them up, there would be more broken glass, dented metal, and piles of ash until it did.

Some of those people may have shed a tear for what was destroyed, but he never lost any sleep over it, that was because most of the businesses that suffered from his hands were far from legitimate. He wasn't burning down an antique shop, he was burning down the front for an unscrupulous dealer selling counterfeit art. He wasn't blowing up a twin-turbine plane, he was blowing up a mode of transportation to import drugs. Exotic sports cars, vacation homes, fishing boats, or wine cellars were all being used as a staging ground for something else, to dupe someone into believing.

The hard bite of bourbon snapped him back to the work in front of him.

The plan was in motion, he had pulled the trigger giving it a green light a few weeks back, and now the people working with him were putting the final pieces together, so they were able to execute it later that night.

To obtain the reference points and information needed to complete their mission, they had already extensively scouted and shot stills of the electric grid they were going to take down located at the edge of the city. As part of their rouse, they eventually traveled to a different substation that had the same general layout and put on a small theatrical play. A few on his team had dressed as the individuals from Persona Non Grata when they went out on their marches. His crew donned the trademark masks and went about acting in front of a video camera, shot from a security vantage point, staging their actions to make it look as if Persona Non Grata were there to take down the power.

Leading up to this, Clive and his crew staked out the substation for weeks on end watching how the guards patrolled the grounds, they looked for any perceived weakness in how they did things, came up with a plan and practiced it until they felt comfortable pulling it off. There was an abandoned building just outside of this target area, that was where they were to meet before they hatched their plot. He was not certain about how they were going to upload the video they shot into the security system, it had him feeling uneasy, but one of his crew people felt they had a solution, and it had better work because it needed to be found by the authorities the following day.

Clive took another long sip of his beverage. He was looking forward to well-deserved down time after this series of missions was over. Closing his eyes, he wished that down time started now, he drifted off until he imagined Tindra standing there as if she were waiting for someone, someone she wanted to see. She was edgy and beautiful, and for him, she was just out of reach, women like that were always out of reach for a guy like him. The both of them were at the opposite ends of the spectrum, of good and bad, of law and lawlessness, and because of that, it was difficult to find middle ground and meet. In his dream he couldn't just come for her, he was frozen, unable to move. However, there was no stopping what was coming for her, call it revenge or a demand for justice, once it caught up with her things would get messy. There would be a very public trial, a dramatic sentencing, and jail time that would probably be accompanied by periods of hard labor. They would be merciless in their punishment of her, but at least she would still be alive. Alive, being alive, that thought had him flashing back to the helpless child in the back of the Bronco and Clive opened his eyes wide out of fear, a fear that somehow if he wasn't careful with how he planned things he could lose Tindra as well. He quickly knocked back the rest of his drink feeling ugly and pitiful. Conjuring up that child now put the energy out there for him not wanting to lose another person, he slammed the empty glass on the table, making for a loud clap, it resonated like a shot.

"No shooting!" He blurted this out in his empty domicile still half asleep.

He kept reassuring himself that he could deliver on this mission, get the agencies message across without hurting anyone, especially Tindra, he was certain of it.

CHAPTER FIVE – CRIMINALS

Tindra woke to the vibration of her cell phone slowly dancing on the top of her dresser. The number to this particular device wasn't one she gave out freely, it was reserved for only those she absolutely trusted, and those were people she could count on one hand. There was a soreness in the back of her throat, and it came to life with every breath she took of the stale air in her room. Rolling her tongue around she found her mouth was raw and dry as if she had been sleeping with it open all night long. Sadly this gave her insight to the cottonmouth her parents would often complain about in the morning when she was younger, and they were still around claiming to be raising her. Testing her voice by humming a few keys of music only proved she needed a glass of water before she could answer the phone.

Swinging her legs over the side of her bed revealed she was still wearing the same clothes from last night. Her black stocking feet poked through the legs of her skinny jeans of a matching color. She might have made it under the covers if it wasn't for the black leather jacket she had on covering her cropped top. As her feet hit the floor, she quickly made her way through her place to wind up in front of the kitchen sink. Lazily reaching for a glass from her cupboard, she stuck it under the cool running water of her faucet and allowed it to fill. It felt good to let her hand pass through the flow, this soothing sensation sent a tingle to the rest of her body, and signaling just how dehydrated she really was.

Seeing her purple nails from her fingers wrapped around the glass brought a smile to her face. For the most part, she wasn't much into fads but had her nails painted in support of her favorite band, the Violet Veronicas. Their pop-punk style seemed to get in the face of anyone wanting to question what they were doing as a group. It was in that vein that Tindra appreciated their take on music, on their reasons for forming the band, and their commentary on life. With the faucet still running, the glass overfilled, and the water cascaded over her hand. She shut it down, tilting it to let some more pour out before bringing the glass to her lips. The cool, crisp, clean feel ushered in a needed relief as it washed down the back of her throat.

The concert from last night was still fresh in her head and had her earworm snaking its way through the library of music contained in her brain, leafing through the catalog of synapsis, eventually finding singles from the band, getting them to buzz with life as it dropped the needle on passages of songs that got her memory to spin out the tune. Tindra had danced all night feeling the up-tempo beat vibing her being. She was almost positive she was one of the last to leave the club having had that much fun. As the water washed the back of her throat, she felt renewed and began moving with the memory of the music, rising on the balls of her feet, stepping with her hips sliding side to side, her head rolling behind what the rest of her body was doing trying to catch up. In her mind the Violet Veronicas were singing:

It's a mistake

to think you can take

all that I worked for
all that I make.

You say I'm a pretender
but you're not so real
so superficial
no genuine deal.

At least I've tried
and it would be a mistake
to touch what I have attempted
don't mess with what I create.

That's when you'd find
my volatile side
with no time for cover
I'd explode like a mine

A powder keg.
A powder keg.
Flash-boom-bang, no time for cover
I'm a powder keg.

Moving to the beat, she was taking in her nail color and was thinking about keeping it, but before she could decide on this, she heard the phone on her dresser buzz once again. Someone was being very persistent, and she was becoming very turned off by their attempts. It was the weekend and she felt she had earned her time off. As she walked back into her bedroom she became aware of a bad aftertaste in her mouth. The water had washed away some of what had built up there overnight but exposed the more determined things trying to take root in her gum line. She rolled her tongue around her mouth in a desperate effort to clean what was in there, she did this little exercise right up to answering the phone in a rather raspy voice.

The person speaking to her sounded annoyed.

"Where have you been? I have been trying to call you all morning!"

"I just got up a few minutes ago, what's going on?"

"You haven't heard? Turn on the news."

"Which channel?"

"Any of them, they are saturating the airwaves with nothing but lies, it's disgusting!"

Tindra rested the phone between her shoulder and head as she got close to her television set and turned it on. It took a few moments for the screen to warm up and show a picture.

"Do you see it?"

"No, the television is still warming up. Can't you just tell me?"

"I would rather you see it for yourself."

The screen came to life and revealed the last station Tindra was watching, a music channel which she quickly switched away from until she got to a block of news stations. The images they were broadcasting were a little chaotic with ambulances and fire trucks littering the screen, The police had a strong presence outside of this loose circle of emergency responders. She caught wind of the newscaster describing the scene midway.

"... a vulgar tragedy that has marked the transition of Persona Non Grata from internet vandals to a terror group. The authorities are still piecing together the terrible chain of events that have befallen these officers, although very little details have been released, those speaking off the record confirm the internet group's involvement. Again, to recap, eight officers shot dead in this abandoned structure in the Weller District."

Tindra almost dropped her phone. "I don't understand, did we do this?"

"Are you kidding me? No way! There is no one within the group that would've authorized this, let alone carry it out, this is all one big mistake."

"Mistake? This has us looking like a bunch of crazed lunatics! Extremists!"

"Some of us are meeting over at the library in about an hour, hope you can make it."

The person on the other end hung up the phone.

Tindra knew he was speaking code to her, the public library wasn't where they were going to be meeting, they were gathering at an online forum site run by a company called Elite Management Systems. This place of business was completely unaware they had been hosting a site for these networking paladins to exchange information for a little over a year now. It was just one in a line of businesses with poor security Persona Non Grata was taking advantage of and who were unknowingly hosting a hidden chatroom or forum for these online vigilantes. To hack their way into those platforms, they had established themselves as legitimate users, free to roam those corporate frameworks until they could establish their backdoor channels.

She put her phone down and went into the bathroom to quickly brush her teeth, if only for the reason of stopping the mild stinging sensation that was developing within her gum line since drinking the glass of water. Halfway through her brushing, the articles of clothing she had on from the night before suddenly felt restrictive, so she began removing them while still in her loo. A small pile formed at her feet until she got down to her stockings, bra, and underwear, it was then that she decided to make her way into the bedroom where she took off those remaining articles in search of more comfortable clothing.

Not wanting to stand out, she began piecing together clothing that were khaki in color. Her underwear, socks, pants, and shirt were a blend of olives, browns, tans, and greys. She found herself dressing in layers because she didn't know how long she would be gone. Getting out of her lair may not have been the smartest thing for her to do, but staying here might even be worse, and she wanted nothing more than to get out so she could think.

She didn't own a motorcycle, but she owned the boots, ankle-high with a thick rugged sole. They were scuffed up from wear, and she found it more of a badge of honor to leave them in that condition rather than trying to keep them clean and polished.

She was working the toothbrush around in her mouth the entire time she was getting ready, working it until a pool of saliva formed in her mouth that she couldn't contain. She rushed into the bathroom and spit into the sink, turning the faucet on to rinse the rest of it out of her mouth. Bending down, she took in a long swig and was letting it run out of the side of her mouth, all the while trying to set her toothbrush down on the countertop. She missed instead and the brush ended up dropping onto the floor. Standing there for a moment she contemplated on whether or not she should throw it out. That's when she heard the jarring sound of her doorjamb breaking apart as the rear entrance was being violently kicked in.

THE AWAKENING

He was scanning the airwaves for any news of the blackout, but the reports weren't coming in fast enough. His patience was wearing thin. His irritation was due to the fact he had slept in, passing out sometime during the evening, never making it out to meet the others. He was trying to convince himself that it was no big deal, the operation should have continued on without him, but deep down inside he knew convincing himself of this was almost impossible.

Clive had come out of his deep slumber feeling a bit out of sorts, groggy up until he saw the ambient light of the grey morning creeping between the edges of his blinds. Seeing the arrival of this new day sent him into an unnerving panic, and he shot straight off the couch he had so slovenly passed out on.

He was leaning hard on the radio listening for information, scanning the channels, and all the while questions for what happened swirled in his head. The biggest story of the day was of some officers being shot, but that wasn't the story he was looking for and so raced right through the reports. He soon found himself leaving this static ridden device for his pager. Pagers were all the rage once again, costing half as much as a cell phone, and a person could text with it. This technology was a required part of an agent's communication platform. He passed through the numbers to see if anyone on his crew had tried to contact him, but there were no new pages. With no one calling him last night he began to feel even more uneasy, the full weight of missing the assignment was beginning to hit him, and his team's silent treatment was only adding to his angst.

He was becoming agitated and could no longer sit at the kitchen table. Grabbing his wallet from the counter, his walkie-talkie to include surveillance earpiece, and lastly his handgun from the top shelf of the cupboard he headed out the door. His intention was to go to where they were supposed to meet up last night, it was the strongest move he could make in the moment. His effort may not have amounted to much, but at least when he caught up with his team, later on, he could actually say he responded as soon as he was able.

Dead silence filled his car as he drove there. He needed it to be this way so he could think, not just about what was going on, but what was going on with him. How could he have been so irresponsible as to have slept through his alarm, he knew the answer but was having a difficult time in confiding in anyone who might have been able to help; but that would mean admitting his drinking was becoming a problem. Out of sheer frustration, he kept hitting the side of his leg, if he could have punched himself in the face with any kind of real intent, he would have unleashed a flurry of fists upon himself. This latest transgression could cost him dearly if he couldn't explain himself convincingly to his team members, word would get out about his dereliction of duty, and as to the possible why's of having slept in. Hell, there was a very real chance his tardiness had already gotten back to his division leader. The clock for this mission was still running, he could feel the beating of his heart racing passed the seconds, the pressure was on, for they would not shut the mission down until he reported in.

The traffic was unbearable in the area, it had to do with the nature of rush hour, there was just no easy way around it in the morning, even if he flashed his badge. The multi-lane highways supporting the city never seemed to be able to keep up with the cars needing to use them. The transportation department didn't seem like they were trying to help, in fact it felt as if they were going out of their way to sabotage the situation with them always fixing an overpass, repairing parts of the roadway filled with pot-holes, or working on any number of ramps, and always at the most inconvenient of times. It always produced a lane closure or the narrowing of traffic into a corridor of fewer and fewer options.

The stalled traffic finally got to him and he turned the radio on only to hear reports of problems for the area he was trying to get into. The substation was situated in the middle of an old industrial complex, with warehouses and abandoned buildings located on the other side of town, so after a while the congestion made little sense. Yet the more he tried to get into that area, the more traffic closures he encountered.

Being hungover wasn't helping with his concentration, there was a ringing in his ears and a queasiness that would come and go in his stomach. It made for thinking about what exits he should take to get around the mess all the more challenging. Suddenly he put the two things together, the reports for the officers down and the traffic closers, they were coming from the same sub-station he was trying to get to.

"Damn it! No, no, no!"

He found himself shouting loudly out of frustration. The shocking realization that his group could have gotten into a confrontation with security or even local law enforcement officers had him reeling. He wondered if they had detained some of his operatives, that would have surely explained the silence coming from their camp. They knew better than to expose an operation once it had been compromised. They were to sit tight until the appropriate response could be taken in extracting them. The agency would start by denying they existed, and they had to. Hell, there were plenty of times where he felt they had denied he ever existed.

He pulled off the interstate and was doing his best to make his way along some of the busy side streets until it looked as though he could no longer drive toward his destination. Emergency and local law enforcement vehicles had set up a perimeter, no one was getting in, no one could drive any closer without their consent. Clive was certain his operation had caused this, and he was beginning to get frightened by how extensive the confrontation had gotten.

Parking his car on the side of the street he began to walk toward the emergency vehicles and barricades. There were plenty of people gathering to get a better look at what was happening beyond the boundary. Peppered throughout the crowd were news vans pulled as close as they could get to the scene with their crews set up outside and reporting. Clive walked as close as he could get and stared off into the distance, into what looked to be the heart of the tragedy and tried to glean any clue as to what was taking place in that area.

One of the newscasters was close enough to where Clive was standing that he was able to overhear their reporting. He was half-heartedly listening to the broadcast, actually putting more energy into trying to get the attention of one of the many officers they had stationed at that end of the street. He was standing there trying to stare one of them down when he overheard the news reporter begin to talk about the casualties.

"...there are a number of fatalities, they won't give us any more specifics than that. Some of the other information they are willing to share with us to underscore the seriousness of this assault is that these were Federal Agents. They haven't stated from which department they were from, but they are saying that all the casualties were Federal Agents. That would explain the massive response to this situation, you have both local and federal agencies descending on this situation. They have not released the names of any of the victims and are still waiting on word about a possible motive. The police are said to have a news conference in about an hour from now..."

Clive felt a chill run through his body until his spine resonated with a pain that caused him to buckle, as he bent at the waist, he grabbed his knees with his hands. Forcing himself to stand upright, he began to walk away from all the news vans and police lines. He departed with an ill feeling growing inside him. As he stumbled away, he tried to figure out who he could call, who back at the agency could he trust to help him with this atrocity, and then that's when it hit him. The agency thought he was one of the victims. That would explain why his division leader wasn't calling him either, they were assuming he was already dead.

He had made his way between the parked cars and crowds of people until he got far enough away and decided to lean up against the brick wall of a building for support. He began hitting himself in the forehead with an open palm.

"Think. Come on man, think. What happened back there?"

He began to go through the motions of recounting how he put things together, his conversations, who he had shared information with. "Who did I tell? Who did I tell?!""

Besides the people on his team, he had only reported back to the agency. The Maryland Procurement Office were the only ones who knew where his team was going to be and what they were going to do once they got there. If the procurement office was assuming he was one of the victims, it was because they knew he was going to be in that sub-station. He got goosebumps along his arms and the back of his neck as he was coming to the conclusion that his team had been set up. If the agency did that, it would mean they had been black flagged, marked for termination, no wonder there were no survivors. On the surface, his next thought made no sense at all, and yet somewhere deep inside his being, it made all the sense in the world.

He needed to tell someone, to find someone who understood what he was going through and might be able to help him, and in his mind that someone was Tindra.

CHAPTER SIX – ON THE RUN

They were running. It was difficult for Tindra to imagine they would be doing this for any extended length of time, but Clive was proving her wrong with every minute that passed as he was on a mission to get them to the edge of town. The motorcycle boots she was wearing didn't make her feet or shins feel good as those thick soles struck the pavement, it was as if they were made of an unforgiving substance, and with each step, she wished she had chosen a pair that would have absorbed more of the shock.

She had so many thoughts going on inside her head as they ran, about Persona Non Grata being named in the attack, of Clive breaking down her door and taking her away, and of how she had been swayed from her small quiet town in the Midwest to the bustle of Boston, all those thoughts were flashing through her mind and making it difficult to concentrate on where they might be going.

Taking a break would have been a welcome relief although there was a part of her that didn't think it was wise for them to stop. Clive wasn't helping, making it seem as if the authorities were personally after them. She was having a difficult time believing that was completely true, how could they be onto who they were and where they would be headed, and so quickly? They had never done anything violent in the past, and she doubted anyone from her group were even at that substation, so how were they going to pin the murder of those officers on her? The things she did with the group in the past couldn't have warranted all this attention, it seemed like a bunch of hogwash, and she cursed the day she had been lured out here to help Nicolas Prin with his term papers. Enough seemed like enough, and she broke away from their timed trot, ducked through the open door of a building they were passing, and into its vestibule where she could catch her breath.

Clive continued on for about ten yards before he realized she wasn't running with him anymore. He came back to find her in the antechamber leaning up against a wall.

"What's the matter? Are you alright? Why did you stop?"

Her hands were on her knees with her butt pressed against the drywall, in this posture, Tindra was too busy panting to look up and acknowledge him. "I am not quite getting why I have to run. I mean I get that they have named the group in the news report, and they say the group has done terrible things, but how does that tie in to me personally?" She slowly stood so she could look him in the eye, not giving up on her support of the wall. "You seem to be the only one here who is in trouble."

Clive felt his jaw locking up as she spoke, his jaw always locked up when things weren't playing out according to how he imagined it. He was a bit of a control freak, he could admit that to himself, and his job seemed perfectly suited for strong personality types. This was probably why he worked solo for most of his time under their employment, and in fact, those in the agency who were proficient in their craft seemed to crave this as well. So, once committed to a plan, he didn't take kindly to its changing or any attempts at diverging from it.

"This isn't some type of game where we get to pick and choose when we participate, people are coming after us, both of us. I don't know that I can make that any clearer to you."

"You've made it very clear, perfectly clear, and maybe that is more to the point because it's only you that is telling me we are both in some sort of grave danger. It's like when a politician puts out a statement and expects us to accept it on its face value. You mean to tell me there is no investigative research on your part? No type of follow up to see how truthful they are being? That's very trusting of you. The news reports I have heard fuel these feelings of being in danger, but no one has named me personally for this crime." She created a little distance between them by walking deeper into the hall of the building. "I can't speak for you, for what happened to your team, but I can surely speak to what I have done, and it is nowhere near the things you are saying."

Clive could feel the heat from his anger building within him, he didn't want to have this conversation, not here, not now. She wanted proof of her having to be on the run, and he couldn't produce it, not until the news reports caught up with everything that went on back at that substation. Not getting his way at this moment also meant he didn't feel the need to be fair or understanding towards her. She needed to learn his word was the law, and in certain situations like now, it was final. He felt the anger surge through his body propelling him forward, closing the gap between them, until he was able to grab her by the back of her upper arm. It was a maneuver used by most parents when their kids were being unruly, and needed to be led away. Even though he had roughly grabbed her by the arm and was now dragging her through the building, he wasn't the one who was intending to bring harm to her, and the only way he could show her that was by proving it to her.

He led her down the hall looking for a stairwell. They took the stairs until they ended up in the parking garage.

Not letting her go even as she vehemently protested and almost took a tumble down the stairs. She could not stop him, he seemed to be headed in a particular direction and all Tindra could do was follow. They crossed the length of the structure passing parked car after parked car positioned neatly in their stalls. They kept walking past all of them until they arrived at an old pickup truck backed into the corner.

Tindra gave Clive an incredulous look. "You can't be serious, really? These things are death traps."

He snickered at her statement. "You have no idea what you are talking about."

She protested. "I most certainly do! I've read the reports, the defects in these larger vehicles are absolutely real."

He tried the doors of the truck to see if they were unlocked and discovered the driver's side closest to the wall was, with Tindra still helplessly in tow, he reached around her to open the door, and then pushed her inside.

Her first instinct was to try the passenger side door, to at least open it and show him she wanted out. As she slid across the seat to do this, Clive climbed into the truck and his leather jacket parting just enough to reveal his body holster with Glock seated inside it. With her hand resting on the handle to open the door, she thought twice about it now, she didn't want to give him an excuse to draw his weapon. Besides, she was too tired to start running away from him and wanted to save her strength for the next opportunity.

"I can't keep holding onto you, and do the things that need to get done. At the same time, you know I can't let you run from me, escaping will only play into their hands, and will do neither of us any good."

Tindra was already suspicious of him and hiding this fact wasn't in her DNA. She was still breathing heavily as she stared him down.

"This is your only warning, don't do anything stupid."

She nodded, and with that, he reached up and lowered the driver's side visor, and then the passenger one. He seemed to be searching for something.

"I don't think anyone is stupid enough to hide a set of keys in their car."

Clive reached to the ashtray located in the center of the dash and opened it, inside was a set of keys. He pulled them out so she could see them. "You might have been right if this were a vehicle they were wanting to keep."

"If we are going to steal a vehicle, can we please at least steal something a little safer, like anyone of the other cars in this port?"

He placed the key in the ignition and started the truck, the starter was slow to respond but finally turned over. The radio came on and was playing country music, Clive quickly turned the dial until he came to a station that was broadcasting the news.

"Trucks like this aren't safe, they just aren't." She was stubbornly shaking her head and looking out the window at the other modes of transportation parked in their stalls as they drove by them.

"It's not going to happen, I'm sorry. This is the vehicle we want." As Clive said this to her, Tindra refused to budge from looking anywhere but out the passenger window.

The broadcast seemed to be at the tail end of a briefing law enforcement was having with reporters. There were plenty of people frantically shouting out their questions, but no one seemed to be responding, and then a male newscaster back at the station broke in. "Well, that was Police Commissioner Dane Hudson filling us in on what information they have on the downed officers in what has been described as an ambush. They downgraded the number of casualties from eight to seven and have identified four persons of interest they believe are linked to the online vigilantly group known as Persona Non Grata."

Another anchor chimed in, a female whose energy for reporting the story was easily conveying the urgency that law enforcement felt, and was obviously reporting from the scene, "Four people of interest the Police Commissioner said law enforcement is wanting to get their hands on and talk to. They haven't come out and told us how they obtained the identity of these four people, but they are saying the suspects have had a hand in the tragedy that has happened here, which some are describing as a massacre."

The report bounced back to the studio.

"As law enforcement continues its investigation, a manhunt is on the way for these four individuals, Brendon Shaw, Alowishus Stern, Timothy Kemp, and Tindra Hightower. If anyone has information on the whereabouts of these four individuals, please contact authorities immediately."

Tindra turned to Clive, looking shocked. "They said my name!"

Clive was still driving, looking slightly concerned by the way she was reacting. "It's what I have been trying to tell you."

"You don't understand, they said my name in conjunction with those murders!"

"I told you we were in danger."

"Stop the truck. Stop the truck right now."

"I can't do that, we have to put as much distance as possible between ourselves and what's happening back there."

"I don't care stop the truck, I'm going to be sick!"

Clive looked at her and saw the panic in her eyes, he had little choice in the matter, that was unless he wanted to drive around with the constant smell of vomit in the truck. He knew no matter how well he cleaned it out, the putrid scent would still be there. He began to slow the pickup down and pull it off onto the side of the road. Even before the truck came to a complete stop, Tindra had opened the door and was spilling out of it. Clive did his best after that stunt to bring the truck to an immediate stop, the passenger side door was still wide open, and when he got out he thought about going around and closing it.

Tindra was moving way too fast and would disappear in the wood line in a matter of moments she wasn't sick, and this left Clive with little choice but to chase after her. As he followed, in his haste, he couldn't remember if he left the truck running on the side of the road or not. On top of this, she was going the wrong way, they were so close to making it to the edge of town before she got out and hopped the guardrail, now this would only add time onto his schedule of them trying to make it out. He moved down the hill keeping Tindra in sight, he ran through the thick foliage of ivy and weaved in between the numerous trees. It was a heavily wooded area, even this close to the road, the dense canopy of leaves high above provided constant shade during the day, and he was grateful for its cooling effects as he ran after her.

She got to the bottom of the hill and found herself at the water's edge. There were few choices from that point, she turned left and headed downstream. It seemed like a fair shot given she could turn in either direction, but soon found she was forced back around to the highway with the trail ending in a clearing where people may have met to exchange drugs, or hang out and do them, or put up a shelter and catch some sleep. Most of the area was hidden from passing traffic, so it was easy to see any of these sorted activities happening there. She frantically looked around for a way out, that was until she saw Clive make his way out of the wood line toward her.

"Stay away from me. I don't know who you are, but you've brought me nothing but trouble since you have come into my life."

She was right about that, but Clive just wasn't going to let her go, not now, nor in the coming weeks. It was going to get complicated, especially if they found her, and it had every possibility of getting even uglier once she was under their control. They had to leave as a team, together, there was no other way for them to make it. He had no doubt he needed her and wished she could see how much she was going to need him. He didn't know if she would ever come to that conclusion, or come to the realization too late, all he could do was try.

"That report wasn't just about you, it's about me too. Those officers back there, the ones that were murdered, they were part of my team. The reason they downgraded the number of casualties was because they finally realized I wasn't amongst them."

"I don't care. I can't. There is a cloud of trouble following you, and I don't want any part of it."

"You're right, there is a cloud of trouble that has followed me, almost my entire life, and I am sorry, but it has found you now as well. The sooner you come to realize this fact, the sooner we can begin helping each other."

"Helping each other? Are you insane?"

"We need to help each other, neither of us is going to get out of this by themselves."

Tindra stood there looking at him for a few moments letting his words sink in. "You're a real bastard, you know that."

Clive had positioned himself between her and the path that would allow her to get away, so it was very important that he stand his ground. "It doesn't matter what you think of me, or what anyone thinks of me really, that's because I have had every one of those thoughts a thousand times over about myself for far too long."

They stood staring at each other for a period of time before Clive spoke again.

"The only way we are going to get out of this mess is if we work together."

"And what are we going to do, where are we going to go?"

"We have very few choices, we've got to get outta here, and get as far away from them, all of them, as quickly as possible."

She was looking him over, eyeing him up, wrestling with her skepticism. "So, what's your deal, were you in the military?"

It seemed like an odd question in the moment, but he was willing to answer it. Military life was tough, it had to be for the people they were fighting were tough, fanatical, most who served came back and just wanted to blend in, to lose themselves in the ordinary. They were fighting wars all over the globe, in places they turned upside down, and in countries that would never have a chance at ever recovering from the destruction. A lot of the soldiers coming home carried with them the guilt of being a part of that. It was something an ex-soldier had a difficult time admitting, that they had a hand in destroying the world, but in this instance, to win her over, he needed to come clean and be ready to talk about it. He nodded slowly at her. "Yes, I have fought in their wars."

"So, is it true?"

"True about what?"

"True about the deserters?"

Clive was stunned in the same way a boxer is stunned from taking a clean shot to the face. He didn't think stories about deserters had gotten back to the general public. He had no desire to talk about that, in fact, anyone who was there and experienced that side of military brutality didn't want to talk about it. There were constant threats, warnings, the policing of platoons, it was all about snitching on friends and bullying people until a thing like accountability twisted in upon itself in the most perverse way. And yes, they shot people in the back that were caught trying to leave them. It was insane, really because not only were the soldiers taking fire from the enemy, they were taking fire from people on their own side. Yet there were those willing to chance it and tried to run away, knowing full well what they faced if they were caught. To them, it was worth it. He closed his eyes for a moment as he gathered his thoughts and hesitantly responded.

"What part?"

"The part where they get shot for deserting. Is it true?"

"Yes. Soldiers caught deserting are shot, either out in the field or after they have been captured and brought back to base. They will march them in front of a firing squad and execute them. I know for a fact because I was one of those soldiers forced to pull the trigger on the firing squad."

"They forced you to do that?"

"Yes, you aren't given an option, they make you do it."

"How? How can they make you do it?"

"If you don't you can wind up in front of a firing squad yourself. Its mob rule, like everything else around here. It's how they've chosen to conduct war."

"I can't even imagine having to be in that situation. I'm so sorry, it must be an awful, terrible feeling."

"Not in the moment, there is no time to feel awful because you are too busy feeling terrified, scared, most are trying to muster up the courage to do it. I had to stop thinking, about anything, and just pulled the trigger when they gave the order. It's afterward, possibly even after you get home from the war, when things slow down and you can process all the chaos that you've been through. When the dust settles and the fog lifts, that's when it hits you, and square in the face."

"Whatever your plan is for wanting to get across the border, what chance do we have if an armed soldier, with all his training cannot escape? What chance do we really have?"

"Well, we aren't in a combat zone."

Tindra let out a cynical laugh, "Bullshit! Have you looked around the country lately, the number of people that have been displaced by natural disasters living in temporary shelters, the daily broadcasts alerting us to the level of terrorist threats. It's every person for themselves. The rich have done that, they keep getting richer and there ain't nothing trickling down. The middle class has blended right in with the poor. We can't take care of the impoverished, our disabled, or the underprivileged. The refugees we are supposed to be keeping out with the large walls we have built hasn't stopped shit, wake up! Those walls are really there to keep us hemmed in. Every year the future manages to look just a little bleaker, a little darker. We're at war alright, with ourselves."

"Look, everyone has some semblance of an idea of what their ideal society should look like."

"Well never once in that ideal do I exist as a freaking fugitive!"

"Neither do I."

"Agreeing with me doesn't mean I then automatically sympathize with you or your cause."

"I'm not looking for you to sympathize with my cause, I hate my cause. I hate what all of it has come to stand for. I just need for you to be in the same corner I am. They're going to be coming after us, the both of us, with everything they've got. Together I believe we offer each other the best chance of eluding them."

"I'll play along, but the first time I don't feel that our arrangement is working, I will leave you."

Clive walked over to her with his hand extended to shake on it. To Tindra the offering felt cold, and she seriously contemplated on what she was getting herself into. After a few moments, she reluctantly put her hand in his to seal their deal.

"I'm not joking, I've got no problem leaving."

"I know you don't. Let's hope it doesn't come to that."

CHAPTER SEVEN – CHISEL

Evening had arrived and they hurriedly made their way to the other side of the parkway. For them to do this they had to cross under the overpass with the only way of accomplishing this was walking through shin-deep water. Clive was the one who insisted they take their shoes and socks off, delivering a dissertation on how the combination of damp shoes and feet would slow them down, and might even cause them to have to stay in one place for more than a day to let things dry out. Tindra acknowledged him just so he would stop harping. Yeah, they needed to keep moving, but she was removing these items for a different reason, the moment of silence that would follow.

As she began walking, she hoped she would make it to the other side without dropping any of the things she was carrying. It seemed a daunting task since she always seemed to lose at least one sock to the dryer on any given attempt. As she saw it, physics was missing out on the big picture, the obvious fact that the rapid circular motion of the dryer drum was causing a disturbance in space-time and sucking socks right out of our plane of existence. Somewhere out there in a higher dimension, the appearance of random socks in one's laundry was possibly as common as pocket lint in our universe. It was either that, or there was a planet out there in the multiverse where socks continually fell from the sky like leaves from autumn trees.

After making it to the other side, they dried their feet before putting their things back on. None of this would have been necessary if they hadn't made their way back to the pickup truck to find a state trooper pulled up behind it, the officer was out and busily giving the forsaken vehicle a once over. Before they could be spotted, they turned and jogged back down the hill to the clearing, then had the lecture on wet socks and boots, until they finally found themselves on the other side of the overpass.

After they got their things back on they started running and didn't stop until they found a place to stay, following the banks of the river they had made it to an abandoned structure, an old brick mill next to a railroad trestle made of I-beams. The lettering on the side was faded, but she could make out the name even as the sun was starting to set -- Watertown Boiler House. The three-story building had been taken over by a population of vagrants and drug addicts. Clive went to work immediately searching, for an area where they could both retire. He wasn't shy about walking through the place, he carried himself with confidence, making his way through the halls and checking out the rooms of passed out and sleeping people. He kept moving forward, working his way up the stairs, until they found a floor that looked to be deserted, this was where they would retire for the evening.

Discovering a large pot in the center of a room wasn't unusual in this structure, it was used to contain a fire, and there were plenty of fires burning throughout the building using Jerry-rigged contraptions like chopped up oil drums and old barbecues. Tindra tried to put herself at ease by surmising this floor was empty because it was too far up into the structure—the others were too lazy, or too blasted out of their minds to traverse the stairs and make it all the way up to this level, either way, she found little comfort in trying to justify it.

Not having a door attached to their room was unnerving, but there didn't appear to be doors to any of the rooms in this structure. Perhaps there was an unwritten rule or unspoken code for those staying here not to violate the small amount of privacy they managed to carve out in this place, but neither Clive nor Tindra were trusting of this unwritten rule and so chose respective corners. Tindra felt a little safer knowing Clive had his pistol but still kept an eye on the doorway watching for whoever might decide to walk through. They had a small pile of scrap wood that was left over from the last user, and Clive would grab a piece from time to time and toss it into the small fire he had started.

"I'm sorry the fire isn't any warmer."

He said this in earnest but Tindra had too many things on her mind to be worried about how warm their fire was. She was still in a state of shock for having given up her cell phone. By no means did she want to do this but Clive was very insistent, and when she finally turned it over to him he went through the process of pulling it apart and threw it as far as he could into the water next to the overpass. Once it disappeared, she felt a sinking feeling in the pit of her stomach, it made her want to vomit, and she still hadn't completely shaken the feeling. The device had a lot of numbers of people she wanted to stay in touch with, it verified that the cryptocurrency she got for various types of hacking jobs hit her account, and it was why she grabbed that phone as she was being rushed out of her place and not the one that woke her.

At least she still had her laptop, grabbing the backpack before being hastily ushered out of her place. The device was uncharged, but all she needed was a little power to communicate with her friends via email, but until that happened though she was in the dark. Which meant she still didn't know anything about the plan Persona Non Grata hatched after being accused of the deadly ambush. She was becoming increasingly curious as to what they may have come up with to get out of this insane situation. There was no doubt they were leaving messages on that secure board, and would become extremely worried if they didn't hear back from her soon. It was the only way she was going to know what was happening with her fellow hackers, when they would next check in, and where they were held up. The not knowing was beginning to tear her up inside, and she needed a way to take her mind off so much uncertainty.

"Is this the plan then, to run from one abandoned structure to the next?"

Her breaking of the silence in the dimly lit room startled Clive for just a moment, he was in the beginning stages of getting comfortable and letting his guard down. Sitting up a little straighter, he let out a long slow breath thinking about her question before he answered it.

"No, I don't think that would work. They will eventually start rounding up all the people in structures like this, accelerate the process in their effort to look for us. A strategy for staying in places like this has a shelf life and will only work over the next few days."

"You're saying they would cast their nets over places like this because of us?"

"It's more to fill the camps they have been establishing across the country, the homeless problem is now considered a national disaster. Contracts were given out to private firms, so they are doing the dirty work with their own security forces. They process the people back at those camps and turn in the ones wanted by law enforcement."

"That's outrageous, I never heard them declare an emergency. I know there was talk of cleaning up the inner cities, but I thought the government was behind the action, doing the heavy lifting, how can they get away with contracting out that type of work? It's a complex problem, and they should be directly involved."

"From what I understand, part of the strategy was based on the fact people are consumed with other issues. They're too busy to be concerned with how the streets are getting cleaned up, just as long as they are getting cleaned. Taxpaying citizens want results. The people coming for us will want results as well. It means more sweeps and raids in an effort to find us so they can cash in on the reward and any other notoriety that may come with it. They'll continue to cast their nets until they catch us."

"There is a reward for turning us in?"

"Most certainly, and if not now, then soon."

"That never crossed my mind. So, what are we to do? Where can we go?"

"I know of a coal generating station several miles from here that I scouted several months ago. I think if we hustle we can make it before nightfall tomorrow and could use that as a leaping off point for whatever we come up with next."

"And just what is that?"

"We need to make it across one of the borders, we have got to get across in some way, shape, or form."

For a guy who spoke of always having a plan, the lack of one now was a problem, and she was concerned their desperation would drive them toward getting caught or meeting an untimely demise. She was hoping for something more concrete from him, something that would shore up her insecure feelings. Clive, however, sat in the corner with the light from the fire dancing across his face. He had a calm about him that spoke volumes to the tense situations he had faced, and each time he made it. This wasn't his first rodeo and at least for now that was enough. The first part of her response could have been mistaken for a sneeze. "Yes, of course, we do, it's how we go about doing it."

"We need to take the initiative, the people they send out after us won't be slouches, but their plans for trying to stop us won't really come together for another forty-eight hours, so we have a little time to figure things out. It's the only way we will really make it. Our first order of business is just getting close to the border."

"We still need to have a plan."

"We will and it starts with the power station. The place will give us everything we need, from transportation to a place to crash."

"And computer time, don't forget, I really need to be in front of my computer."

"I imagine you'll have plenty of time to do that because I'll be scoping out and commandeering one of their utility trucks."

"A utility truck?"

"Yes, I don't think they'd look for us in that kind of vehicle, especially not one representing the power company."

"No, it's not that. I'm sure you're right. I don't understand your fixation with pickup trucks. Vehicles like that have proven to be unsafe. Knowing our luck, it will fail us when we need it the most just as they are prone to do."

"That's not true."

"The hell it isn't, there have been plenty of reports, it's well documented, they've caused serious accidents, people have even died in them when they've failed."

"Not true." Clive blurted this out well above the normal tone of conversation, it was clear he was getting upset, and it caused Tindra to clam up. After a few moments had passed, he regained his composure.

"It's simply not true. I can't explain it, but there is nothing wrong with the pickup trucks themselves."

"That goes against the grain of everything that is out there. Do you know something we don't, or is this just a feeling of yours?"

"Utility trucks work, don't they? I mean, that's why they have them. They use them to complete jobs. How can those trucks work at utility companies and the others supposedly don't?' No one ever thinks about the fact that the utility companies, construction, the national guard, and the army all use trucks like this. I get it, those trucks aren't really seen when they are in use, but they are still being used."

"I'm no expert, I don't know trucks, but I thought the vehicles you are talking about were different. They weren't made for ordinary people."

"So, utility trucks could be safe then."

"I guess they could be."

"Well, that's exactly what we're stealing."

"It seems like stealing anything will only raise red flags and draw more attention to where we could possibly be."

"How will they know we stole it? We won't be leaving them a note. Besides, we are still in need of a conveyance to get us around, making our way on foot isn't going to cut it in the long haul. A vehicle would put some real distance between us and whoever decides to give chase."

"I still don't like the idea of it."

"You're going to have to trust me, it's our best option."

Getting that utility truck to save them from walking was one way of selling it, but Clive had a more selfish reason for wanting that particular type of vehicle, it gave him access to a communication device, a citizen's band radio or CB. The information he was operating on was old and would expire within the week. He needed a way to listen in and retrieve any updates as they were being made available. Other agents would be doing this as well, communicating with each other over those frequencies and when they did they used code words and he had insight with those codes. A bang and burn operation, carnivore targets, OSINT hubs, and validated pocket litter for districts that were under martial law was just some of the information being transmitted, and he needed access to it if they were going to stay ahead of the game.

The small pause was broken by Tindra, who was still looking to keep her mind off things. "Even if we were to make it to the other side of the border, how do you know the government of that country won't turn us back in?"

"They won't."

"Another hunch?"

"No, that's a fact."

"How can you be so sure, with all that is going on out there. Countries aren't as welcoming to foreigners, not with all the travel restrictions, limited visas, and border crackdowns. Can you blame them with all the wars and disasters looming off every coast and horizon? Look at what's happened at a place like Fukushima, every year they have to admit the disaster was greater than they first reported. They've gone as far as trying to freeze the earth around the plant to prevent groundwater from seeping into the lower levels of the reactor and turbine compartments. That's been a failure ever since they've turned that frozen barrier on, forget about the cleanup, they can't even get to those deep areas, all those radioactive materials are trapped underwater, and when they pump it out, it simply fills up again. All they've been doing is storing pumped contaminated water on-site, over a million tonnes of it, water no one will ever be able to drink, and to top it all off they're rapidly running out of room.

That disaster alone would be enough to ask where everyone is supposed to go to get away from it? But no, we have plastic islands of garbage so massive they are breaking apart at the molecular level and getting into the seafood chain, and that is on top of the already high levels of mercury that exists in sea life. The bleaching of coral is only a reflection of how much ultra violet light is getting through our thinning atmosphere, people around the world are really starting to feel the heat. I hate to be the one to wake you up to these facts but that is only a small fraction of what is causing the chaos enveloping this world. All this concern and friction over mass migration is because of these unsustainable conditions along coastlines and along the equator, but no one ever talks about that.

And you know what really makes me sick? The endless diversion of money and resources away from anything good we could be doing, ripping it away from cleanup projects, our infrastructure, our health as a people, and growth as a nation, all in support of war. My god, we are at war with everyone, if we would have just taken that money and time and fixed problems like hunger, disease, and pollution when we had the chance we could have saved this planet, saved countless populations and did it cheaper. Look at the price we're paying now. We hide behind our walls with a seemingly singular purpose of destroying everything outside them when we had the power all along to make things right. No wonder most of the countries out there despise us, what have we really done to help?"

"I'm sure it seems that way. It's the message the government has been pushing -- *everyone hates us*, but the people of those regions, the actual citizens, really want to help those who are trapped behind our borders."

This wasn't the first time Tindra had heard this argument, and she had done her research, reading the blogs about the supposed groups out there on the other side ready to aid and assist. Unfortunately a lot of the times the ones reaching out over the internet wanting to lend a helping hand were individuals paid by the government to monitor its citizens, and they went out of their way to set these citizens up, trapping them with their dreams of escaping. When they were caught, they were made examples of, paraded around and put on display through the official media outlets as traitors cooperating with a foreign power.

Tindra squinted as if she were trying to get rid of those thoughts. "It's been my experience that if they're out there, they are awfully hard to find."

"It's not going to be easy, I never said it would be, this is going to take lots of hard work on our part to make it happen, but it's why I'll need your help, and it's also why you'll need mine."

She gave him a slow, extended nod. He had been communicating with her, trying to be open, and she was appreciative of his attempt however misguided it might be at times. She had been through plenty of secured servers in the past, been in plenty of forums that were set up for those being squashed by the rule of law, and she was always surprised at how many of those chatrooms were being used by citizens from within her own country. Those users would often rant about the tactics used in repression, hypervigilance, and the claimed battle against extremists. They railed against the government for perpetuating conflicts to keep their people down, using the threat of global warming in keeping them pent in behind tsunami barriers, or illegal immigration to keep people behind huge walls at the border. The mass surveillance programs supposedly meant to keep them safe from hostile threats but were really used to peer into the lives of their own people. It was for this last reason she hated exchanging ideas online with anyone she hadn't already gotten to know, there was just too much to risk, and it didn't exactly endear them to her when someone went out of their way to try and engage her in conversation, she usually shut them down.

Clive followed up on her last comment. "You said they were hard to find. I'm curious, have you ever contacted any of them?"

"The short answer is no, but there have been hints of movements, shadow entities outside our borders trying to reach the citizens of this country, who claim they want to help us escape. Even though I want to believe in it, I can't really put any stock in what they're saying, anything that feels even remotely like clickbait I try to avoid. The internet can be such a dangerous place."

Clive nodded in agreement, grabbing some scrap wood and threw it in the pot to keep the fire going before retorting.

"Baiting people is part of their scheme for testing the population, misinformation is another, and yes, from what I've heard Big Brother is trolling the internet, always looking for those that might be leaning toward leaving, getting away from what has been mandated by the administration. They do the same thing with their agents, testing them all the time, making sure they are still loyal to the cause. It's all about conveying a knowing, putting their feelers out, finding the ones sitting on the fence, those that have the nerve to question what is happening in this country and getting them to react. I try never to respond to that kind of energy."

Clive's eyes were wide now, as if he were expecting someone to walk into their room.

Tindra gathered herself a little tighter, bringing her knees to her chest, squeezing them with her arms, as if she were gathering her energy.

"I once worked for a businessman, helping him organize the financial records for his many endeavors out of his home office. He was a wealthy executive who had some sort of side business where he was renting equipment back to his firm. He was making money hand over fist, so much so that he saved it in different accounts and places offshore. It didn't exactly seem legitimate. He was trying too hard to hide too many line items within his books, and I think even for a while he was hoping after I found some of this out that I would stay on as his bookkeeper. He compensated me quite well, but I just couldn't fall in line with that. It seemed so risky, and I felt if he ever got caught, I would become the fall person. There was no way I was ever going to let that happen, but it didn't stop him from trying."

As Clive listened he could relate to this wealthy gentleman's intent at keeping Tindra around, he had broken down a door to get to her, and he had no doubt if given the opportunity this executive would have done the same.

"He had a chisel he used to keep in one of the drawers of his desk. It was old, beat up, but eerily clean as if he actually cherished it. The tool looked as if it were manufactured during a time when being a handyman was a honorable profession. This rugged implement seemed odd in a drawer full of paperclips, pens, erasers, scotch tape, even scissors. It stuck out like a sore thumb but was there none the less. I would think of it from time to time, trying to imagine why he had one tool like that in a drawer full of office supplies."

Now Tindra's eyes were turning into big dark circles, telegraphing a haunting energy, one she had most definitely experienced before. This all was being personified by the light of the fire and made her look as if she were in some sort of trance.

"And did you ever figure out the mystery?"

"When the job was over, he presented me with a gift, a necklace with a small amulet attached to it. He called it a Caelum." She reached up and undid the top part of her jacket, and then the top few buttons of her shirt, she reached around the back of her neck and pulled the necklace up over her head, balling it up in her hand. She got up and walked over to where Clive was sitting and handed it to him.

He unfurled the chain to see what it looked like, even as he did so, Tindra could not help but describe it to him.

"It's a quarter of a circle as if the bottom part of the globe were cut off and hung by its points on the necklace. That is the symbol for what is known as a Caelum which he told me means heaven. Sometime later I found out a Caelum could also mean a chisel. When he gave it to me, he said that he hoped it would remind me of my time with him and that one day he hoped I would understand that this heaven was out there waiting for me."

Clive stared at the necklace until he realized Tindra had stopped speaking, she was standing there, waiting until she had his full attention before finishing her thought.

"I have never told anyone that story before, but I think I have figured out a few things since then. The chisel he had in that drawer and this quarter circle are symbols meaning the same thing, they either represent a resistance or a freedom, maybe both. I think the Caelum are an actual group on the other side of our border. I believe some of the money he was diverting to those offshore accounts was to help fund them. I think they are out there on the other side of the border waiting for someone like us to contact them."

She left him holding the necklace as she went back to her corner and sat down. Tindra could see Clive had his doubts, he was processing the information, probably much like she had when she first started putting the pieces of this puzzle together back when she worked for her boss. There was nothing more she could say that would convince him tonight. He would have to deduce this for himself just as she had.

"I think this is one more reason for getting me in a place where I can use my laptop, so I have a chance of reaching out to them and establishing some kind of contact."

He was staring at the necklace, studying the symbol, trying to think if there was any time during his travels that he ever saw someone else wearing something like this around their neck, or even something so random as a chisel lying in a drawer full of office supplies. He looked over into the corner where Tindra had taken a seat once again.

"We've got to make contact."

"I never had a reason to until now. Sometimes surviving is enough, and that's what I've done up to this point in my life, but it doesn't mean I haven't looked into it or been tempted by the possible ways to get a hold of them."

Clive found himself nodding in agreement, he had survived plenty up unto this point in his life as well. Now he too was looking for a way to get out, away from all the madness.

His attention came back to the necklace. The small symbol of the Caelum hung off the chain as if it were a large bowl capable of holding so much more than things like resistance and freedom, perhaps within its sloping walls, it also contained a thing called hope.

CHAPTER EIGHT – THE POWER STATION

As Tindra was about to find out the following day, Clive would not take a direct route to where he wanted to go, or at least not a direct route that lasted for any length of time, he put this kind of effort in to avoid detection. She could appreciate the idea of it but she was usually employing those methods seated comfortably in a chair, typing away on her keyboard as she covered her tracks, erasing histories and clearing out caches all in an effort to stay under the radar. Physically having to follow through with such a strategy was a far more arduous task.

He was in possession of a map, and that moved her to be a little more onboard with his strategy of zig-zagging across the state. He was doing his best to keep them off any of the roads or highways, so even the bridges they crossed were more pedestrian or rail in nature. Sticking to this technique the probability was high of them running into a train, he conceded that, but if it were going in the right direction, could put them in position for making it to Worcester.

They had spent part of the day marching up along the river and away from the bay. It was a grueling trek because Clive kept leading her away from the shoreline to have them walk more in the wooded areas within its low-lying banks. The route wasn't always well-defined, and they spent some of their time either attempting to clear their own path or going around obstructions. Anytime it got too complicated they would make their way to the top of a hill to reassess their situation. They had to back-track twice to get around hazards they saw no other way of negotiating. Anytime it got too complicated they would make their way to the top of a hill to reassess their situation.

The Charles River is a winding body of water that carves its way from Echo Lake to Boston Harbor, it doubles back on itself more than once as it makes its way through the heart of Massachusetts. For that reason, short cuts were developed, a series of trails that were connected by hiking enthusiasts and the locals residing in the towns the path passes through that cut from one point on the river to another instead of having to follow the entire arc as it flowed. The Charles River Link Trail, as it was known, started in Newton and cut through Wellesley, Needham, Natick, Dover, Sherborn, and ended in Medfield. Tindra was very grateful that Clive chose to use it at times, as the path allowed them to both make up for lost time and not have to think about how they were going to traverse uncharted ground.

About a mile before the trail ended in Medfield, a set of railroad tracks crossed the path, and they graduated from the trail to following the set of tracks heading in a Northwesterly direction. They were tired and hungry but were also clear on what they were trying to achieve and so continued to grit it out. Fortunately for both of them, Clive had a packet of water purification pills, and an olive-drab covered cylindrical canteen, so at least they were able to stay hydrated.

They approached their walking along the tracks the same way they first began hiking along the water's edge, they were close to it when they needed to be, and when they could, they'd disappear into the wood-line or on the other side of a row of bushes that would separate a field from the rails. The walk wasn't bad, and before she knew it, they were at the fringes of the rural city of Farmingham.

She really wanted to go into town with Clive and duck into a coffee shop, plug her laptop in and let the battery charge. She didn't even need to use it and would have sat there with a warm cup of java looking out the window until he was finished running whatever errands he needed to run. Clive would have none of it though, so Tindra ended up staying out at the town's perimeter, finding a tree to sit under just off the railroad tracks, there was a clearing beyond the tree-line filled with wild grass, and that was the side she chose. On the opposite side of the tracks was a lot with different piles of dirt, the mounds were tall with some of it being landfill, gravel, and other forms of rock or dirt. The occasional noise of heavy machinery told her it was an active yard and another reason she should stay away. It was the perfect amount of quiet where she was but could hear the bustle of business happening in different areas around her, that white noise was just what was needed in helping her fall asleep.

Clive made his way into the antiquated town, its boxy architecture and tight feel for spacing unfolded before him as he walked the streets scoping things out, looking for what might be available in aiding them on their journey. He was gone a little over an hour and a half before he was back in the presence of Tindra, she was sound asleep leaning up against an old broad-based tree, and he wrestled with the idea of waking her. She looked so peaceful laying on her back with her arms spread as if she had surrendered to this rest without a fight. He knew he had pushed her just to make it to this point, he might have let her catch up on more sleep if it wasn't for the fact he had returned with submarine sandwiches from an Italian pizzeria. He had ordered a meatball sandwich and a hero sandwich, a couple cans of soda, and a small plastic container filled with pepperoncini.

He personally wasn't concerned about surveillance, nor anyone spotting him out on those streets, they weren't looking for him the way they were looking for Tindra and her friends. To have that kind of liberty to move about would help them in getting around early on in their avoidance. He knew it wouldn't last forever though. Eventually, those back at the agency would think of some contrived charges in which to frame him as well.

He kicked the bottom of her boot. She woke with a start, sleepy and bewildered.

"Hey, I brought us back some food."

This news brought a warm smile to her face, and she sat up, straightening her posture, stretching and yawning until she was sitting up against the tree.

"Oh wow, that smells delicious, what is it?"

He knelt down in front of her and opened the bag, pulling out the sandwiches and the container of pepperoncini, she chose the hero sandwich when it was offered. He sat down across from her, and they opened their respective meals and ate.

"I scoped the town out, there isn't much of a police presence, so I think it will be alright if we go in for an errand or two. I saw an army-navy store in town. I thought we would go by there and pick up any supplies we might need, small backpacks, any food items they may have, t-shirts, underwear, dry socks, a packet of moleskin, hand towels, toilet paper, anything that might make our journey a little easier."

She responded between bites, "I have a backpack already."

"Well, what if you can't fit everything you want in there, maybe it's a tote."

"Maybe if I can't fit it in my bag I don't need it. How about some bicycles or a set of wheels?"

He snickered at her sarcastic response as he placed his sandwich carefully on its wrapper, and reached for his map, "I think I have that figured out. Just on the other side of town, there is a small switchyard where lines of boxcars are usually picked up and dropped off. There should be something going our way, so I thought we'd hop a ride."

Tindra looked hopeful at the prospect of transportation, she nodded enthusiastically as she chewed the last few bites of her food, finishing her sandwich. Taking a long swig of soda to wash it down, she brought her other hand to her tummy and let out a long slow burp. Clive glanced up at her a little shocked.

Addressing this, Tindra was rather nonchalant. "What can I say, cola has that effect on me."

She relaxed back against the tree as lunch was obviously settling into her stomach, delivering the after-meal knockout blow.

Clive seeing this laughs a little. "Hey, hey, hey. Don't go falling asleep on me."

"Can't we just relax here for fifteen more minutes?"

"I guess we can do that, fifteen minutes, just don't get too comfortable." He said this with a smile but meant it.

Twenty minutes had passed, and they were finally on their way to the Army-Navy Store, walking into town, Tindra broke off and darted into a drugstore. It caught Clive off guard, and he went in after her. Not wanting to make a scene, he was walking close behind her, trying to keep up, talking as they made their way down an aisle.

"What the hell do you think you are doing?"

"I needed to come in for a few items that might not be at the Army-Navy place."

She was in the feminine hygiene section perusing the products. Clive was looking uncomfortable the entire time she did this until she finally reached for a package of tampons.

"They have video cameras all over the store. Anyone searching for us will have a record of us being here."

She wasn't letting his attempt at scolding affect her, still carrying herself with ease as she made her way over to where the gift cards were.

She batted her eyes at him. "Stop acting like we're out of place and it won't be such a problem."

She reached out and coyly grabbed a handful of cards and slyly put them in her pocket. Clive seeing this reacted.

"Are you crazy? Those don't work unless you put money on them activate it."

She shot him a knowing look. "No shit Sherlock."

Getting to the register, she paid for the tampons and then made her way out of the store with Clive in tow. Once outside, he reacts to her going into the drugstore in the first place.

"Listen to me, you can't just go where you please, especially when I've done our homework to make sure we won't be detected at any point in our excursion."

"That may work for you, but not for me. I'm in this situation too and need to take care of myself."

"By stealing gift cards? How does that work?"

"How about getting us to the Army-Navy Store and I'll tell you a little bit about it."

As they made their way across town, Tindra explained how she would remove the sticker on the back, record the code, and get new stickers to place over what she had removed. The secret was getting it back on so that it didn't look as though the card was tampered with.

"And that's it?"

"Well, not exactly, I have to register them online. Usually, I would have them send me an alert to my phone when a person puts money on the card, but someone threw my phone in the river."

"It had to be done. There was no way around it."

"Well, I'm going to need the ability to purchase things, with my own money, and this is one way we can do it. I'll just have to rely on my laptop to notify us.'

Framingham has more than its fair share of automotive prospects, and Tindra felt she saw most of them as they made their way through town to eventually be walking along the rails again after being in the Army-Navy Store. In certain spots there was a distinct smell of automotive grease, diesel gas, and car exhaust. There were junkyards, a pick-a-part lot, small establishments that dealt in the sale of used vehicles, an auto mall, businesses that sold parts, as well as transmission, engine, and collision repair shops, it was as if they had hauled a portion of Detroit down here on one of the trains and the whole thing jumped the tracks spilling the contents all over town.

After crossing an under an overpass further down, they made their way a few hundred yards to a small wooded area between a self-storage facility and a lot where they parked public transit buses. The small switch of five tracks lay before them, and they waited there for an engine to come by and hook up to one of the many lines of cars sitting on those rails.

She was nervous, not like she had been the night before staying in the abandoned building, this nervousness was about energy and timing, it was about making their train as it pulled away and without being spotted. They had extra weight on them now, with their backpacks full of supplies, socks, underwear, toilet paper, and some Ready-Made Meals. She never had a Ready-Made Meal before, and Clive told her she was in for a real treat. She doubted his sincerity, but it mattered little for if her last day traveling were any indication of what lay ahead, the meals would be happily eaten with no complaints.

They waited in the shade of those trees for a couple of hours before they heard the sound of a train engine approaching. It took a few hours for the engine to be hooked up to the cars, the men working that yard had walked the line several times, making sure things were safe before they allowed for the train to leave. Clive and Tindra waited until those cars started down the tracks before they made their move, hopping in one of the boxcars toward the end of the line.

They threw their backpacks in first and ran along-side the car as it slowly picked up speed. It wasn't easy because the ground under their feet wasn't as level, they hit loose gravel, dips in the surface, and the occasional beam supporting the track all in their attempt to jump inside. Tindra made an effort to get in the car first and halfway up was pushed in by Clive. He then raced along-side and made a smooth transition getting into the car. Tindra had taken a tumble and was laying on the floor when Clive climbed in.

"That last push was a little uncalled for, I was going to make it."

"I just wanted to be sure, I guess I'm just used to a faster pace for things getting done."

"Oh really? Like breaking down my door, if things aren't moving along, you force them?"

Clive was uncertain if she was joking or not, "I guess so."

She stood and dusted herself off, "I will keep that in mind the next time we hop into a boxcar."

Clive grabbed both packs and went to the back of the car.

Tindra watched him sit down with them and was taken aback as he went through the process of trying to figure out who's bag was whose. He then went into his bag and began laying things out so he could see them.

She walked over to where he sat, grabbed her bag, and made her way to another corner. "I take it you have never been married?"

The question caught him off guard but knew his behavior around her must have been a complete tell.

"No, I haven't, why would you say that?"

"Just an observation that's all."

Clive saw she was visibly bothered, and he really didn't know what to do about it. He wanted to make her feel safe, but he also wanted things done in a timely manner, to execute the plan, whatever the plan was in the moment. It was tough to convey his feelings for this kind of exactness without sounding harsh, "I can't change who I am."

"I wasn't asking you to."

"But you were implying something about me, either unrefined or rough."

Tindra sat in the corner looking at him, knees bent so that her forearms were resting on them, she had a loose grip on her bag with one hand.

"I think there has been a lot of implying going on. Law enforcement officials have implied that I am involved in something despicable, you have implied things as well, breaking into my house long before I even knew I was in trouble, you imply we should be moving faster, but you don't have a real plan, so there is a lot of implied energy floating around and I'm sorry if some of that implication has fallen squarely on your shoulders."

"Look, I can't apologize for who I am . . ."

Tindra let go of the bag and shot to her feet, she moved toward him talking a little louder, making larger hand gestures, her growing frustration with Clive was obvious. "...and maybe you should. Maybe you should start apologizing because not apologizing has only gotten you in the same situation I am in. Maybe you rubbed someone the wrong way back where you worked, maybe they were waiting for an apology that never came, and when you kept on crossing a line with them, they had enough and actually tried to kill you. That's what you have been telling me, right? Someone tried to have you killed, so maybe, just maybe being who you are isn't the answer in all of this. Maybe there is a window that should be opened in your world in which civility is allowed in like the air we need to breathe because you know what, that is what I'm used to. They might not be after you right now, and you might feel the need to move quicker than we have to, but you know full well I have done nothing to deserve being thrown into this boxcar."

They may have been moving down the tracks, but she was standing her ground. Her face was flush and stern, she wasn't giving in until he acknowledged what had been said, she may have been coming off as unyielding, but she was beautiful, nonetheless. He didn't understand how he could be drawn closer to her after just being scolded, but he was, so he said the only thing that could be said in a situation such as this, "I'm sorry."

"Oh no you don't, you don't get to go there. Don't even think by agreeing with me I'm not going to be mad at you."

She turned her back on him and walked to the other side of the car, to create some distance and to lean up against the slats. He watched her for a moment thinking about what she had said, the stand she had taken, and how because of all of it he was becoming more and more infatuated with her. He stood up and walked over to her, placing his hand on her shoulder as he delivered his heartfelt apology.

"Hey, I am truly sorry for doing that. I don't know what gets into me sometimes. I just see something that needs to be done or that I am trying to accomplish, and I attack it. I am not saying that is always the right thing to do, I just know there are times, plenty of times when I need to be a better man."

She turned slowly as he was talking until she was facing him. "I'm tired."

"I'm tired too."

"No, I'm tired, so tired of it all already, the running, the trying to stay one step ahead, their accusations, It's all such nonsense."

He reached out and put his hand on her shoulder, and with it they began to fall until they were seated, leaning on each other in part because it felt safe, but also just to be touching. This was more in support of each other than anything that could have been misinterpreted as passion and it was easy for both of them while doing this to doze off.

The train entered a tunnel, and the echo from this quickly pulled them out of their slumber. Their only illumination came from the warning lights for the trains using the long passage. He knew where they were and wanted Tindra to know so they would be ready.

"We are under the city of Worcester."

LEAPING OFF

The coal-burning power plant sat close to Indian Lake and just off of Highway 190 looking like a prison without the guard towers. It was a blockish looking building with smaller square structures of varying sizes shooting off the main pile. Within the large yard were two long and narrow smokestacks positioned diagonally and on opposite corners from each other. A giant white cylinder looking object jetted up from the center as if it were a silo. The large brick walls that formed off the north end were built to support another adjacent yard, and this one was filled with mounds of coal. Knowing it was a coal-burning power plant did little to ease her anxiety about the place. The last thing she wanted was to be in there snooping around and then get hemmed in by law enforcement. The both of them would be trapped like rats. These may have been her concerns, but they weren't Clive's. He was focused on getting the things he wanted out of this facility and had no intention of being caught, which only added to Tindra's anxiety.

When the train slowed down as it made its way through an s-curve, Clive and Tindra jumped off, putting themselves between the tracks and Highway I-190. Even though the train was moving at a slower pace, the speed with which it was traveling fast enough that both of them had to tuck-and-roll as they hit the ground. As Tindra did this, her backpack flew from her grasp and popped open, dumping its contents all over the ground. Clive had jumped up and spun around, ready to make a move toward a small group of trees when he glanced back to see what had happened.

"That didn't go exactly as planned." Tindra said this after she had situated herself to be sitting on the ground. Clive made his way over to help her up but she waved him off, rotating her shoulders and arms in small movements, making sure everything still worked properly. Once things checked out with herself examination she got up and joined Clive as he was picking up the things that had popped out of her backpack. She started by taking the backpack from Clive and reaching inside for the laptop. Opening it she checked to see if the screen was cracked.

"Do you think it will be okay?"

"I'm not so concerned about the internals, it has a solid-state drive, and by all appearances the screen looks good."

"I guess we dodged one there then." Clive said this with a smile, but she wasn't feeling his luck.

"Laptops and the rest of this stuff we can always replace. We have a long way to go before we start dodging things of any real consequence. I think I'll save whatever luck I might need for that moment."

"You're right about that." Clive shook his head as he stood up and stopped to scan the grounds of all her stuff, and before he knew it he was just standing there and staring at her possessions.

Tindra caught him doing this and paused picking her stuff up. "What's the matter?"

"I don't know. This reminds me of being overseas, in one of the many urban combat zones. The garbage strewn about, everywhere, endlessly being blown about, it's everywhere. I don't know if they can ever clean it up. It's all turning into one big dump."

"Eventually, someday, someone will clean it up."

"I wanted to believe that, I wanted to think it could be cleaned up, but it can't. Every country we fire armor piercing rounds in, every one of those that misses its target and hits dirt has some amount of spent uranium embedded in the ground, and we are talking about years and years of uranium being accumulated in their soil, seeping into their water table, the same one they use for drinking and their crops.

Tindra collected the rest of her things and quickly made her way over to where he is stood, shaking him out of his trance. "I know what you're saying is important, but we can't afford to think about that right now."

"There is so much garbage, it's so trashed. I can't see how they are ever going to clean it up."

"Maybe we should take cover in that line of trees over there." Tindra grabbed him by the hand and lead him over to a spot they could sit down. They waited in the shadows as Clive slowly snapped out of his trance.

"I lose myself sometimes, with things I've done in the past, I guess things I'm ashamed of or feel guilty about. It seems the older I get, and the more time and distance is put between me and what I've done, the more I'm haunted by it, does that even make sense?"

"They are your experiences, so of course it does."

"There is no escape."

His last words resonate with her, framing her feelings about what is happening to them now. They sit there in silence watching the plant, watching how the trucks pulled in and out of the parking lot, the timing of the workers that came and went from the main structure and adjacent lot with trailers serving as temporary offices. They sat there watching and waiting until the sun went well over the horizon.

"So, how did you find me?"

"What do you mean?"

"I am talking about you crashing through my door and snatching me out of my place of residence. You can't sell me on the fact that was coincidence or happenchance."

The question gave him reason to pause. He knew at some point she would be asking this, it was a poignant fact connecting them, and it was inevitable. The fact it was happening now might not be the best timing for what they needed to get done. The power plant was in sight, and they really needed to make it inside. On the other hand, if she didn't like his response there really wasn't a way to contain her, and she would leave just like she promised. This was a make-or-break moment between them and lying wasn't going to help. If he lied to her now and it was later discovered, he knew it would spell instant trouble for him. He took a deep breath and gave as straight an answer as possible.

"The government has had you and your group under scrutiny for some time now. Evidently you popped up on someone's radar, someone high enough up the food chain that they saw your group as a threat. My team was given the task of setting your group up and painting Persona Non Grata in a bad light."

She jumped up from where she was sitting and shuffled away from him. "You set us up? You're responsible for all this? For making us look as if we're murderers?"

He slowly stood up, he didn't want to frighten her away with any sudden movements. "No, it's not like that. I didn't do that. We were supposed to make it look as if your group had taken down the power grid for a section of the city. We were to create blackouts over the next few weeks through acts of sabotage and computer hacking. It was supposed to look like your group was behind it."

"My god. Who did this? Who ordered this to happen?"

"Now that I cannot even begin to answer. The Maryland Procurement Office is so big, expansive, maybe a director of operations, a splinter intelligence group...shit, it could be a port security official, our organizations are so intertwined through the sharing of information it's hard to say where one bit of intelligence is obtained, or who goes over that data and then makes a decision on how to act on it. Intelligence gathering doesn't mean there is any amount of clarity on who is behind the gathering."

Tindra was panting heavily, fists clenched, looking at him with all the energy of a wild animal defending what little turf it had left. He could see how enraged she was becoming and had to try and quell it if they were to press on with what they needed to accomplish. He approached her slowly, hands raised.

"The mission was never designed to hurt you, we were only told to discredit your organization."

"Discredited? Jesus-Mother of Mary it's gone well beyond that, there are people out there who think we are killers. What you've done is totally irresponsible. You're all crazy!"

She turned and began marching away, Clive seeing this chases her down, grabbing her and spinning her around roughly.

"You aren't the only one they're after, hell at least they aren't shooting and killing people on your team."

"Not yet!"

"Look, I hate this has happened to you, never in my wildest dreams during my time leading up to what we were doing did I ever see this coming. That should be obvious!"

Tindra began striking the middle of his chest, it was an all-out-assault with her clenched fists.

"Why us? It's such an injustice! All I have ever done is fight injustice, and it seems the harder you fight it, the more injustice they dump on your lap. It's a fucking frightful world of injustice."

She was becoming visibly exhausted by her outburst, she had given so much of herself already, she had very little left in the tank, especially now in resisting his presence. Seeing this, he took advantage of her weakened condition, pulling her in until he was holding her close, his arms wrapping her in a warm embrace. It was then that he felt her physically surrender.

"I'm sorry. I am really, truly, sorry for this happening to you."

They stayed that way for a few moments before Tindra got her energy back up. She got agitated rather quickly and pushed him away.

"We gotta go. We gotta get into that power plant so I can warn the others. You have got to get me in front of my computer now."

Clive went back and retrieved both of their backpacks, he then returned to where she was standing and handed one of them over to her. "Let's get to it."

He turned and trotted off toward the power plant, Tindra wasn't far behind, she wanted to pace herself and reserve her energy, they still had so much to do.

An Instance of Opposition

CHAPTER NINE – THE HACK

Tindra sat under a desk in the dark room, her eyes fixed on the screen of her laptop as it booted up. The desk she was hiding under provided a shield for the light from the computer screen, preventing it from illuminating the room and drawing the attention of a passing guard or curious employee. When her home screen finally revealed itself, it was of a photo of a tropical beach made of smooth white sand, the ocean water was a glowing turquoise, and the calculated shot was devoid of any people. As Tindra dimmed the screen, she caught herself becoming transfixed by the image. She tried to picture where such a beach might exist. If they let anyone out on those smooth sands to feel the cool water as it raced up onshore and washed over their feet. It was either that or the beach was completely off-limits, just as the picture portrayed, a conservation area they were going out of their way to protect because so much of the world's beaches were disappearing under the rising tides caused by global warming. Breaking the spell this photo held over her, she interlocked her fingers and reversed her palms, so they were facing away, and then extended her arms in a slow stretch that brought her fingers to life for typing.

She and Clive had crept into one of the uninhabited construction trailers, there were a few to choose from, but the one they decided on was definitely shut down for the evening. After the last employee left, and they watched him drive away from the crew parking lot, Clive made his way in and swept the area, making sure it was empty. He left her in there to try and accomplish her goals as he went back out to investigate their chances of getting a truck. There were several parked in the lot next door, and he reckoned to attain one it was only a matter of finding if they hid keys on any of them. Before he snuck out into the yard to begin his search, he had given Tindra strict instructions not to leave until he got back.

It was unnerving being in that dark under a desk knowing that only a few trailers over was a group of nightshift employees. She feared at any moment one of them could come into her trailer looking for a file or wanting to get away from their fellow employees to complete additional work. To get her mind off of this, she dug through her bag until she found the gift cards. There were eight in all. She went about carefully liberating them from their cardboard envelopes. After removing the sticker on the back of each card, she went about creating eight new email addresses, and then eight accounts on the gift card company's website, registering the cards. Usually, she would have set it up so her email alerted her phone of any cash added, but that option now lay at the bottom of a stream.

She used a note taking program to record everything she had done so she could recall any info she needed on the cards. Reaching into her backpack, she pulled out the silver reflective tape and razor knife she purchased at the Army-Navy Store. She then scoured the room for a ruler and hard surface to cut it on, like a book or tablet. Finding the ruler, she set her sights on a series of encyclopedias, grabbing a thinner volume and returning back under the desk to finish the cards out.

Once the tape was cut and affixed to each card, Tindra went about logging out of the browser she was on and to a more surreptitious way she could move around the web. The new browser she called up had File

Transfer Protocol command functions. Tindra didn't like the feeling of someone being able to monitor her movements on the web, and any ordinary browser would definitely do that, but there were still ways to access the internet without using one. FTP was a way to text commands, as was done early on with computers to review filesystems, or in her case access, the web.

She immediately went to work addressing an online data tool she had parked the previous year on an unsuspecting remote server. Tindra got this information from an ex-employee of an up and coming cellular phone company. This upstart business had banks upon banks of servers running all the time, backing up content, storing information, and having programming dumped onto it every single day. It was a trove of data that the company wasn't in a position to manage. Things were happening at such an explosive rate they hadn't thought about auditing the content. She had paid a hefty price to gain access to this framework, but was willing to do this to have a platform that wasn't associated with her.

Now in this dark trailer, she was burrowing her way into those servers and accessing the program she had parked there over a year ago. Most of the players at Persona Non Grata were funneling their usage through a much more secure system that had been developed by the United States Naval Research Laboratory and was now run by volunteers; it was called the Tor Network. This network catered to the idea of anonymity on the web and was a mainstay for most who were looking to operate that way. There were a few in Persona Non Grata who were thinking about moving toward what Tindra had done, backdooring a bank of servers at an unsuspecting company and hiding an anonymity browser within. That was because there was talk of Tor becoming compromised, of the government attempting to breach the inner workings. Those rumors were playing off Tindra's paranoia now, and with the information Clive had provided her earlier in the day about the government monitoring their communications, she felt somehow her friends' might indeed be compromised on this network.

Once access was confirmed and her data tool activated, she cruised the web looking at newsfeeds on Persona Non Grata. After reading through some of the stories, she found a news article about Clive. It reported how he was a surviving agent from the massacre, that they had lost contact with him, and how they thought he had turned rogue and joined forces with Persona Non Grata. It concluded that he was definitely a person of interest in the case, armed, and dangerous.

The State wasn't pulling any punches in the press, none of the accused were getting any breathing room. They were snuffing their voices out, dictating the narrative in the media even before one of them had a chance to tell their side of the story. This was all the more reason she needed to contact her friends.

Tindra reached the chatroom where she was supposed to join them the previous day, logged in, and read the posts meant solely for her. She could sense their panic, their disorientation from all the press coverage, and their desperate attempts at trying to reassure each other in this critical time. She also gleaned from their conversation that it was imperative they develop a plan. Worries were mounting as to the cost of any plan they came up with. They also felt it was important they made contact with her, they were becoming very concerned, wondering if she had run into trouble, or perhaps even caught by law enforcement.

As the thread continued, she read where Brendon stepped up his game and took control of the conversation. He began planning and organizing their escape. His inspiration for this seemed to come from a reliable contact, one outside of Persona Non Grata, one he had built a rapport with that worked at the border and now appeared to be aiding in their efforts to slip away. Near the end of the thread was a message addressed to her in which specific instructions were given. She was to go to Crane Beach and take a utility road just off of Argilla Highway before it loops back onto itself at Castle Neck. The utility road lead south for about an eighth of a mile to a small pier. A privately-owned boat would take them from there to just outside a tsunami wall where arrangements had been made for them to eventually get on another boat, a commercial fishing vessel that was permitted to go beyond the border of the country and head out to sea. This was their plan for going north and eventually getting outside the controlled territory.

They were to meet at the Ipswich at Crane Beach within two days of the writing of the thread, and they wouldn't be posting anything else on the board unless they decided to abort the mission. She leaned her head back for a moment and thought about the timeline—in two days from this writing, that meant tomorrow evening.

"No, that can't be right. They're rushing into this."

She wanted to type an entry in to have them stop what they were doing, to have them quit their plan, but in doing so, she didn't want to give away the fact she knew the government might be monitoring them on the site.

On the other hand, if she planned on joining them she would need money, lots of money, more money than she was going to get from any gift card scam, and she would need it by tomorrow.

"Think damn it. Think! I need to finagle my way into some type of financing."

Her whispers were quiet shouts in the dark, echoing under the desk until the word *finagle* started to play upon itself, *finagle,* turned to *weasel,* and *weasel* turned to *worm,* with the word *worm* finding some resonance within and reminding her of -- Nicolas Prin. What was he doing now? She typed frantically, searching the web for him and then his name began popping up. The more she dug, the more she found. He was working as a Procurement Officer as a government resource agent. He must have been good at what he was doing because he was recognized by his superiors and awarded for it. He was married with two children and living in a gated community deep in Virginia.

She did a quick search through the files she had on her computer about Nicolas. In her many dealings with him, she had slowly gained information about his banking to include his user name and password, routing number, his account number, his ATM card number, and pin. Those few afternoons where she used his computer at his dorm room downloading and completing his papers allowed her to collect a majority of this banking data. It was backed up on her computer in case he ever decided not to pay her for a job she completed. Now she was staring at the file and wondering if it all those numbers still had relevance.

The Eastern Block Bank page was up on her screen in an instant, and she rapidly entered Nicolas' user name and password. The page gave her a swirling little circular symbol in return to let her know it was looking for her request and then his banking paged popped up. She was in and quickly started going through his records. They were littered with monthly deposits followed by cash withdrawals at casinos and the racetrack, purchases for items at liquor stores, gas stations, and bars.

"That son-of-a-bitch. He's got an account, separate from his wife, I'll bet she doesn't even know about it."

Tindra looked to see how much money she could transfer at any one time from his account and then thought about the paper trail this transfer would produce. There weren't too many places she could go with this idea without it leading back to her, and that was going to be a problem.

Suddenly she heard someone approaching the trailer, shutting the laptop rather quickly, she nervously waited for what might happen next. The door swung open, and she heard Clive call out to her quietly. She responded by opening the screen on her computer. Seeing the ambient light softly bloom from under the desk, he made his way over having closed the door behind him and knelt beside her.

"What have you found out, are your friends alright?"

"I've got mixed feelings about that." She was busily searching for information about Nicolas' wife, Maria. Tindra's eyes darted across the screen until she was able to obtain their home address.

"I need to complete a few more tasks before we go, it should take me about fifteen minutes. Can we spare that?"

"Yeah, we are good to go. I found a truck we can use, the tanks are full, and it looks to be in pretty good shape."

"Okay, while I'm finishing up here can you put those gift cards back in their cardboard holders?"

"I thought you were activating them?"

"In a way I have, now we just need to wait until someone loads them with cash."

"I don't get it."

Clive began shoving the first one into the sleeve, it wasn't going well as he was mangling the cover. Tindra seeing his rough handling of it reacts.

"Wait, stop what you're doing."

"What's the matter?"

"You need to put them back, so it doesn't look as though the card has been tampered with. It's the only way we are going to get anyone at a store to purchase them. Understand?"

Clive looked her over once and could tell she meant it.

"Okay, I'll be mindful in putting them back."

"Thank you."

She stated this with some frustration as she went back to the computer and to the banking page. If she was going to withdrawal cash from this account and not have it lead back to her, she would need to pull one hell of a ruse. Finding the *manage account* tab, she added his spouse as a signature to the account. She then closed the page and typed out an email to an acquaintance she knew that specialized in false identifications. She requested one with her photo and the name of Maria Prin on it. Tindra included the address she wanted on the card and asked for a forged credit card in this woman's name as well. She then gave her contact the precise time and place they were to meet. Closing her email, she informed Clive of her plan.

"We need to go to the Arsenal Yards tomorrow."

Clive stopped what he was doing. "What? That's in the complete opposite direction in which we want to go."

"No, it isn't because we will be headed for Crane Beach after that."

"What? Crane Beach? What the hell for?"

"That's where my friends said they are going to be. I've been out of touch with them for too long, and their plan has been set into motion."

"Who told you this?"

"It doesn't matter. What does matter is I'm also going to need to borrow some money from you, cash I'm going to need to help me with my plan."

"The hell it doesn't matter, it most certainly does, and don't you go thinking that if you keep asking for things that I'm going to get overwhelmed, give in and grant them to you. We'll talk about your cash needs in a moment, first tell me who told you to meet at Crane Beach."

"Brendon, he is a trusted associate and well connected in our group. He knows how to stay on top of things like this. He's got it all figured out. He even has a contact that is helping him arrange their escape."

Clive didn't say anything, and in that sudden silence, he wished he had met Tindra under different circumstances, one where they actually got to know each other like two normal people, but instead he felt a sick uneasiness begin to creep into his stomach. This was happening because of something he had set into motion, and long before he had ever met or even taken a real interest in Tindra. He could have never imagined what he had done playing out in this fashion, and now here it was coming back to haunt them. His jaw drooped, exposing a section of his lower teeth, his tongue appeared thick as if it were blocking his airway. His eyes were locked onto a single spot in space somewhere well beyond where they were sitting. He let out a slow dreadful moan as if he was trying to figure out how to begin.

Tindra became concerned.

"What's the matter?"

Clive snapped himself out of the gloomy haze he was in and blurted out the first thing that popped into his head.

"Commandant2600."

"What did you say?"

"Commandant2600, that was Brendon's handle, his user name wasn't it, in the group?"

Tindra was caught a little off guard by this and responded in a defensive tone. "Yes, it is his user name. How would you know that?"

"Because I received background checks on each of you when I started the assignment, the information was pretty detailed. It felt as if they had been watching you for some time. That lead my team to set up our plot around power outages and blackouts. It was one of your people, Timothy Kemp, that gave us this inspiration, he was constantly googling information on power grids and substations. We needed an in, one that wouldn't tip our hand about what we were doing, and we felt contacting Timothy would have been out of place, possibly even signaling our intent, so we needed to find another way in."

Clive thought about getting them to start heading to the truck, to get them both moving, perhaps it would deflect some of what he was about to say, but her expression said she wasn't going anywhere until he finished telling his story. "In setting up our operation, one of my team members was able to reach out to Brendon, feed him information about things that were happening within the community, the internet community. Information that concerned weakness in mainframes at different corporations, back door entries he could exploit, internal networks that were set up without safeguards like firewalls, or codes that would allow him into a T-1 line, data trunk, or fiber-optic network. Anything to gain his trust so we could influence him later on when hatching our operation."

"Did this contact say he worked at the border?"

"Yes. We came up with a cover that had him reading Telex information of what the government was getting updated on, only he was supposedly feeding it to Brandon as well."

"Your people are still setting us up!" Tindra was fuming as she tried to get up, but Clive reached out and grabbed her by the arm, holding her down, keeping her in place.

"Listen to me, the team member that was doing this passed away in that ambush. He's dead. The man is dead."

The hold Clive had on her arm was hurting her, and the frustration she was feeling for this situation was coming to a head. Tears began to flow as she tried to put it all together.

"I don't understand. What are you saying?"

"I think someone back at the agency, or the authorities are using his handle now to influence Brendon. They've obviously gotten ahold of my work on this project and have now talked him into walking into a trap."

"Let go of my arm, you're hurting me."

"I just want you to believe I never thought I was hurting you, any of you."

"But you have, you have set my friends up, you have set them up to fail, and maybe even worse."

Clive looked at her and shook his head, "I'm sorry."

"We're passed all of that now. I just want to gather my things and go save them."

They stared at each other for a moment as he let her go. Clive flashbacked to the woman stuck in the Bronco sitting on the rails. He could see it all so clearly as if it were happening all over again only in some strange way, this was his chance to go back and make amends, to save someone he had a hand in setting up to fail. He closed his eyes and began to nod in agreement.

"You're right. We need to go back."

CHAPTER TEN – CHANNEL CROSSING

There was something about driving at night that made the trip seem longer. Perhaps because, other than road signs, there weren't any other noticeable landmarks one could see. It helped in sending Clive's mind on an endless loop thinking about all the possible outcomes that might happen if they made it to Crane Beach, if the rest of Persona Non Grata were going to be there, or if law enforcement had indeed laid out a trap.

Tactically the plan wasn't working for him because there was only one way in or out when driving to where they were supposed to meet them. Passed the road where Brendon and the others said they were going to depart was a huge parking lot known as Castle Neck. This would be the perfect staging area for policing agencies to set up their operations and lie in wait. Anything this big would be a joint effort, with local, state and federal agencies taking part, and that parcel of land could easily handle being used as a staging area for this.

He shook his head as if to shake off the image he had in his mind of driving through the roadblock that leads to Castle Neck and pulling up to see all the mobile trailers, the observation and eavesdropping equipment, and the abundance of officers in tactical gear. They would have officers staged on the fringes of where

Brendon and his crew were to meet, waiting for them to pull up by that little dock off of Argilla Highway. The entire location sat well away from any populated area, which only gave Clive even more of a rotten feeling for what may lie ahead. If he were in charge, planning to try and capture them, this is exactly where he would ask them to meet.

Clive glanced over at Tindra, she had fallen asleep as soon as they hit the parkway. They had been pushing hard and all of it was taking its toll, their running and now her friends being set up, the stress this was loading onto her system had to be unbearable. The longer they succeeded in getting away, the more stress there would be, the harder they would need to push; by the time this was over, they would undoubtedly be running on fumes. The sound of the wheels making contact with the highway let out a loud, low hum. It was the type of white noise that was hypnotic and probably the reason Tindra was able to sleep so soundly. To Clive, it most certainly sounded like a noise that was building to the climax of their disjointed journey.

DOUBLE TAKE

Tindra leaned into the counter of the fast food restaurant with her hands turned backwards, pressing down through her palms so that she lifted herself until she was standing on her toes. Even as the young cashier took her order he sensed something was out of place, but he couldn't quite put his finger on it. She was clean, fit, and attractive, which made her food order of a large burger, fries, and beverage almost unbelievable. Although there was a part of him that could picture her grabbing the to-go-order and heading straight back to her place to play video games. Nothing could have been further from the truth but that was usually how people viewed her, steep in suspicion, under rating her capabilities, and undervaluing her as a person. Even to the young kid taking the order knowing something was out of place, she didn't acknowledge his staring, and as soon as the order was in the bag she was out the door.

Clive saw her approaching the truck and still couldn't get over how beautiful she looked. The morning had brought plenty of surprises, and they had certainly pushed the barrier on getting things accomplished. His one caveat was getting the money she wanted to borrow from him as far north as he could drive in an hour and a half of time. That's what brought them to the Belknap Mall in Laconia, New Hampshire.

While he went to an ATM to withdraw the cash, she went to a drugstore and purchased a limited amount of beauty supplies, this modest purchase helped in distracting from others she outright stole, and during all of it she managed to plant the gift cards she had taken a day earlier back on an appropriate rack.

Afterward, they met by a restaurant that hadn't opened yet, crossed the street to where a Goodwill Store was located and went through the tree line to get to their truck. All the while they were doing this, he was still questioning the chances of her plan had of working. The only reason he even went along with it was the continued use over the citizens band radio of the code word 'poison apple.' If that word did indeed pertain to them, then she might very well need an independent cash source.

There was a clothing outlet a few miles down the highway heading back in the direction they needed to go and was their next stop. He pulled off onto a side street just before the outlet and into the entrance of a drive-thru restaurant. The entrance serpentine its way into a parking lot supporting the fast-food establishment, but Clive pulled off onto a convenient dirt patch before it and parked.

"This is it?"

"This is as far as I can take you. I feel I'm in the perfect blind spot for the restaurant. You'll have to hoof it from here."

Tindra rolled her eyes. "Well gee, thanks a lot."

As she exited the vehicle, he called out after her. "Hey, if you can, when you comeback could you grab me a burger and fries?"

His request was met with no reply as she headed toward the restaurant and disappeared inside. She was gone for twenty minutes before she returned, holding a bag with his food order. Seeing her approaching, he was taken aback, she had washed her face and hair, applied some foundation and lipstick, ridding her of the grit and grime of their dogged travels. Her skin looked young and fresh again, her hair untamed and flowing, and all of it yielding to her prepossessing nature.

He searched for a comment to give her as she got closer, but they were all sounding cheesy in his head, and he took a pass on it when she tossed the bag of food into the truck along with her sweatshirt and jacket. Sporting an olive drab t-shirt, the jeans and her biker boots she was already wearing, she somehow looked different, confident, unafraid. Leaving him there with his burger, she went off to get her outfit for the bank, when she picked up her false identification and credit card a few hours later at the Arsenal Yards, her acquaintance did a double-take, not believing it was really her. Tindra took it as a compliment and a good sign that her plan just might work.

BANK ROLL

Tindra found herself in a branch of the Eastern Block Bank looking to withdrawal funds from Nicolas' account. She was nervous, to say the least, the palms of her hands got clammy as the teller she had been dealing with called over one of the representatives from the floor. He left the comfort of his desk stationed in the middle of the room to come to her window and after a few moments of conversing with the teller and looking at the screen, escorted Tindra back to his desk where he was now reviewing the account on his computer. He had her two forms of identification laying out in front of him on his desk, this was the test they had been created for and she was hoping they were going to pass, especially having just picked them up a little under an hour ago.

She wasn't sure what felt more uncomfortable at the moment, the fact she was sitting there sweating it out with what was going to happen next with this banking representative as she tried for the withdrawal, or the new heels she had on to compliment the outfit she purchased in order to pull this stunt off. The thinly strapped high heels were a half size too small and made her feet feel cramped in their bindings, which caused her discomfort but were the closest in that style they had in her size. She had to have them though because they were the perfect complement to the dark charcoal, modestly cut mini length dress she was wearing. The outfit was topped off with a tight-fitting blazer of the same color that covered her long sleeve crop top and bare shoulders. The sunglasses she had on made her look as if she hadn't a care in the world, she was the perfect combination of sexiness and power, with her shades giving the feel of being straight out of a celebrity magazine.

She needed this look if she was supposed to be the wife of a government resource agent. The outfit wasn't cheap, to say the least, and on top of it, she had to borrow the money from Clive, who she felt wasn't completely on board with what she wanted to do. Possibly because of all the errands they had to run to prepare for this stunt, and they had started earlier in the morning to get them done. It was as if he were bracing himself for what was about to come by standing outside of their parked truck, looking the part of a utility worker by wearing a safety vest and hard hat. He was wavering after hearing Tindra plead for what she wanted to add to the list of things to be done and where she needed to go.

"Well you're not asking for much now, are you? You have to pick up an outfit after we go to the bank? What happened to Crane Beach and saving your friends."

"This is a part of the process, and the more we bicker about it here, the less time I will have in getting to the places I need in completing my tasks."

"And you want it all done before noon? It's almost laughable."

"Not as laughable as you in all that safety gear." She may have looked the other way when whispering this, but he was meant to hear it.

"As long as we have this truck, this is what we're going to have to wear in order to maintain a low profile, and that's just one of the challenges facing us."

"Well, I won't be caught dead in that crap."

"And I hope you don't need to wear it because that would mean we've fallen under someone's scrutiny. Here's another problem we might be facing. I know you would like me to loan you some money, I'm just wondering, can I?"

"What do you mean?"

"To this point in our trip I've been using the cash I've had on me. There is no doubt they are waiting for some type of transaction to happen on one of my cards, that is if they haven't already shut them down. When any of those cards show activity, they will respond by sending teams in to investigate, that means them going through surveillance footage and sending up drones to blanket the area I last used them in."

"So, how are we going to get around that?"

"If we are going to get the funds from my account, we should do it far away from here, as far as we can drive in an hour or two, so if they do come after us, they will be in the wrong area."

"If they have been monitoring Persona Non Grata, don't you think they might be anticipating us going to Crane Beach and meeting my friends?"

"Possibly. You said you didn't respond to any of their messages, so there is a chance they think you still haven't gotten them. Either way, driving north for an hour or so and getting the money there can't hurt us, they might even think we are continuing to head north straight for the border. That would divert some of their resources away from where we intend to be."

"Well, what are we waiting for?"

As they drove, Tindra began trying to think how she was going to get to her friends without the government agents detecting them. She was regretting not having reached out to Brendon the night before and warning them not to go. At the time, it seemed like she was risking much if she did, but now she was thinking it was worth the risk, especially with the passing hours and her feelings they were being set up.

Clive interrupted her thought process. "I was monitoring the CB traffic as you were sleeping, I started hearing them refer to an operation entitled 'Poison Apple.' I think that pertains to your friends and Crane Beach."

"Poison Apple? Why would they call it that?"

"Who knows, they tend to think of crazy names for missions."

"That's it? A crazy name. That's all you got from it?"

"It's a crazy name because of what it infers, the poison apple, you know, when you take a bite from it you go to sleep, silenced."

The banking representative was breaking the silence between them now, he was asking her a question, wiping away the memories of her morning, pulling her from the fog she was in. When no response came, he repeated the question politely.

"So, your husband added you to the account last night?"

"Yes, on line. We had a huge talk about it yesterday, and he finally admitted to having the account which he has hidden from me. We have kids, we have bills, and his hiding of this money isn't helping us."

"Yes, I understand. How much of a withdrawal were you looking at again?"

"Ten thousand."

"I think that's part of the problem. You see we, don't give out more than five thousand in cash on any given day."

"Well, that's a shitty policy."

"We could transfer the funds directly to your account ..."

"No, that won't work because I have bills I need to take care of today, a lot of it includes paying off a personal loan I took from one of my relatives that I want off the books immediately. Look, I had this argument last night with my husband, I don't want to rehash it all over again with you. All I know is that it's only fair that the money comes from this account. Why is that so difficult for everyone to understand?"

The banking representative could feel how uncomfortable the situation was becoming and the tension that was mounting following her comment of rehashing an argument between the couple from last night. He thought for a moment before throwing his hands up in mock surrender and returned her two forms of identification by sliding them across the table.

"Okay Mrs. Prin, I can see you've been through a lot, and I don't want to delay you any longer. I'll walk you back over to the teller, and we'll complete your withdrawal."

The small embossed purse she had purchased could barely contain the money, but she managed to cram it all in, finishing the task by throwing the flap over and locking the clasp. When she exited the bank, there was a part of her that wanted to run and a part of her that felt relief, the most relief she had felt in a while.

NO ROLLING BACK

It had been a long day, and when Tindra woke, the truck was parked in a quiet residential area. She wasn't quite sure where she was, how long she had been sleeping, or where Clive had gone but, by the look of the dimly lit grey-blue sky it appeared to be early evening. The overcast that was accompanying it didn't feel as if it were going away any time soon. The window on the driver's side was rolled down a few inches, allowing for the smell of saltwater to seep in with the mist of cool, damp air. Listening, she could make out the sound of waves rolling up onto a shore.

This sound was a calling, of something primal within her, of wanting to be free. She wanted to write in her journal, write about how conflicted she was about being with Clive, how torn she felt about not being with her friends, and how upset she was about the lies they had put out there that was ruining her life. Her desire for this would go unfulfilled for she realized she had left her journal back at her place. All of her thoughts, her hopes, dreams, fears, suspicions, hatred, loves, and lusts were chronicled within those pages. Her heart sank with the thought of losing that book, and she wanted nothing more than to go back and retrieve it.

She rubbed the sleep from her eyes and sat up straight in her seat. Looking forward through the somewhat fogged windshield, she could make out Clive standing on the beach. High grass accompanied the border of a trail leading out to where he was standing and framing him perfectly out on that gentle dune.

As she opened the door, she got a real sense for how cold it was, and for a moment thought about closing it and waiting for him inside. For whatever the reason, that didn't feel quite right to her, for they had come too far and so she went to him.

Now standing outside the truck, from what she could infer, they were parked at the end of a street. The houses that existed there were set back from the road with lawns full of thick rich and rugged green grass. Large trees with fat trunks that eventually spider out into giant canopies of leaves as they reached up toward the sky seemed to accompany every house along that row. The size of those trees spoke immensely as to how long they had existed, and how long this neighborhood had probably been around. She saw rows of shrubs, partially built fences, and walls of stone that tried to help define the borders of each lot, not that it mattered much with the lawns running into each other as soon as the wall crumbled or eroded away, seamlessly merging the properties as if they were all part of one giant lot. It was beautiful in the way a peaceful meadow in the middle of a forest is beautiful.

She made her way out onto the coarse sand, with each step she could hear the crunching of it under her strapped high heels. She felt oddly guilty for adding noise to the otherwise peaceful morning and so took the time to remove them.

Clive heard her approach and, without turning to look at her, spoke.

"Did you get some good rest?"

"I suppose so. It was a little disorienting waking up in the truck."

"I am sorry about that, you were knocked out, and I didn't want to be the reason you woke up." His gaze was fixed as he kept staring out across the bay and at the landmass that was on the other side. "Besides it gave me some time to scope things out."

"What's over there?"

"Across the way is Crane Beach, and the hill to the left is Castle Neck. We are on the north side looking south, the dock where your friends will supposedly be is on the other side of that hill."

"I don't understand, why are we over here?"

"Because I don't believe your friends are going to be there." He turned to face her, "And if they are, well they've already walked into a trap, so why should we?"

Tindra didn't know what to say. She was still trying to gather her bearings. She looked to him for help. Clive could see this and responded.

"I have been watching that hill, and there is more activity than there should be at Castle Neck this time of the evening, it's as if they are gearing up for something big. Between the sounds of the waves washing up on shore, I could hear a generator running, the warning noises heavy vehicles make as they back up, and the movement of lights, lots of lights, from vehicles and flashlights. There are a lot of people over there, a lot of people."

"Then we need to go and warn Brendon and the others."

"I know that feels like the thing we should do, but there is no guarantee we would get out of whatever trouble we found ourselves in. It's quite possible we would all be caught. I can't see it ending like that for us, besides this isn't your area of expertise, moving about surreptitiously is how I've made my living. I am the one that needs to go over there and warn them...or save them."

"And what? Leave me over here by myself."

"I wouldn't be, not if your friends are over there at that pier. We would simply get on the boat they say they are going to board and come back for you."

"And how long am I supposed to wait for you before I realize that isn't going to happen?"

"You won't be." Clive walked over to a group of kayaks on the beach.

"I'm not getting into one of those things; you struggle a lot to move very little. Those have never been my thing."

"And I wasn't asking you to get into one. It would be counterproductive to everything we are trying to do."

She watched as he walked over the kayaks, making it to the other side of them to where a stand-up-paddle board rested, "This is what I want you to get on."

He gestured to it as if it were some magical device she could stand on and fly away. She was resenting the implication that she wasn't good enough to go with him. It didn't sit well with who she was, and she let him know it. "I'm not getting on that thing either. You want me to float around out there on the ocean until you come by and pick me up."

"If you want my honest feelings on the subject, I don't think it's going to work out that way at all."

"What do you mean?"

Reaching into his pocket, Clive walked back over to her. "It's time you take this back." His clenched hand hovered above hers until he opened it and the necklace she had given him back at the mill dropped into her hands.

"The Caelem? And what am I supposed to do with this? Hold onto it until you return?"

"Maybe, I don't know. You're a smart girl. You'll figure it out."

Tindra was in disbelief, she walked away from him and toward where the stand-up-paddle board was with her heels in one hand, she gestured with the other. "You can't be serious. You're expecting me to stand on that thing and paddle my way to where? Freedom?"

He stood there staring at her, refusing to give any ground. His posture for this wasn't making her any happier. She exploded with outrage. "You think this is some kind of joke, a game? You said it yourself, these people will kill you if they get the chance."

"They most certainly will."

"If you're right about all of this, then if you go over there you will be giving them that chance! Don't you see that?"

"I see that as one possible outcome, but I don't see it having to play out that way at all, you're not giving me enough credit. They have turned the tables on all of us, so many times now, I plan on returning the favor, and in kind."

"Against all of them? No, I won't let you, it's too damn dangerous."

He walked over to where she was standing and grabbed her by the shoulders, shaking her a little, bracing her as if she were a mark. "This isn't your call. I have to do this. If your friends are over there, they're in danger, I can help them, and then we'll be back to pick you up…"

"…and if they aren't?"

"And if they aren't, well I guess then we will know about a whole other set of circumstances now won't we."

She broke away from his clutches, "That's just crazy talk, what we should be doing is looking for another board so you can come with me."

"To what end? Even if I did make it over the border with you, I would only be endangering your life further. It's one thing to have a citizen defect from this country, it's quite another to know one of their own, an operative from the government, has made it to the other side. They would most certainly hunt me down, have me extradited, or worse yet, have me killed."

"For God's sake, no one says we have to be public figures when we get to the other side."

"It would be nice to think things could work out in that way, but I'm afraid it would be different for me, there wouldn't be any peace, not after our side figured out where I had gone. The people over there would have questions for me, of course, they would have questions. Wouldn't you want to know the mindset of a government which goes out of its way to trick its citizens, to get them to believe in something that helps those already in power to stay in power. The camps they have created to house people, the controlled borders. Hell, the judges they have stuffed in the high courts, the ballot boxes they stuff at each election, and no one can do a thing about it. Protect and Serve doesn't mean protecting and serving the people anymore, it means protecting and serving those that have control, those that want to retain power. It's such a mess. It's such a godforsaken mess."

Clive rubbed his face for a moment before he continued. "Look at us, look at what they have done to each and every one of us. They tell us we are living in the most powerful nation on Earth, the land of the free, and the home of the brave. Is this really what they would have us all believe? All the big money, the greed, the elected officials with too much power, there is no rolling back the clock now, we can't snap back to a time when families were more important than a company's bottom line. Social Services and supporting infrastructures designed to help people in need, departments set up to protect its citizens have all been rendered powerless, and in their place are things like hatred, misinformation, financial hardship, and the idea that corporations have more rights than people. It's whatever they can do to enslave a society, it's all being watched, we are all being watched. It's inescapable, an unblinking eye."

They stood and stared at each other for a moment as if they were searching for the next thing to say. Tindra began backing away, her eyes ablaze, and focused only on him.

"It's rumored the most dangerous place on this planet is locked away deep inside the destruction of Chernobyl, under the confines of the new safe confinement structure, beneath the damaged Sarcophagus, there is an artifact called the Elephant's Foot. It is the lava from the core that has seeped down into the lower levels of the plant and hardened there in the form of this animal's appendage. Even though it is no longer molten lava, it is considered hot, probably the most radioactive thing on this planet, if you were to stand next to this hardened lump for more than thirty seconds you would most certainly die within a few weeks. Knowing that, knowing all of what I know about that hideous crystalline zirconium silicate, why does this environment feel more toxic?"

Clive pointed at the necklace that was draped over the end of her hand, "If they exist, if the Caelum is real, then you need to find them. You need to find them and hide away so you can spread the word of what you know."

Tindra was scared, and he could see that now. She never asked for any of this, but if she ever wanted to make a difference, if she ever wanted to find likeminded souls that cared about what was happening in this world, this might be the only way.

"What about Brendon? What about my friends?"

"Either they are in custody, or they are still on the run, but if they are over there, I will find them. That symbol you hold in your hand, the Caelum, it represents a belief, a hope, and you need to be that right now for all of us. The old chisel in your bosses' drawer, that's resistance, and that's what I need to call upon when I cross over that channel to discover what is going on over there. Each of us has a role now in what we should be doing to move on, to go forward, to make our way out of this mess. Each of us in this moment represents an instance of opposition."

"'Tis better to bend than break," Tindra whispered. The wisp of her words took on an unmeasurable strength.

A quiet followed as they stared at each other, each taking in who they were and what they needed to do.

CHAPTER ELEVEN – CASTLE NECK

Clive greeted the nightfall in the full uniform and tactical gear of a law enforcement officer. He came across his new wardrobe quite by chance when the policeman in question had wandered near him to take a leak. The officer had walked into the woods to relieve himself, and as he was finishing up, Clive ran up from behind and struck him. The officer went flying down the hill, it happened so fast the officer never even had a chance to yell.

Landing down by the shore, the officer was knocked out cold. After stripping him of his uniform, Clive cuffed him to a tree.

He still couldn't believe he had rowed his way over to Castle Neck in a kayak, he doubted he would ever get in one again. With every stroke of the paddle through the choppy Ipswich River he realized Tindra's assessment of this small watercraft was correct. He was putting in a lot of work for very little payoff, it was not only that, but his lower body, his hips, butt, and legs were all trapped within the small craft that often felt well below the waterline. The buoyancy of the craft made for an uneasy feeling, bobbing about as if he were going to capsize at any moment, and anytime a mistimed wave hit his craft he thought he was going in, but he kept fighting, paddling hard to stay afloat and eventually was just a few strokes away from shore.

Any place he wanted to land was a rocky unapproachable mess, with fallen trees whose long trunks were waiting to be cut into logs, or big patches of thick mud, or the tall growth of grass in lock step with this wooded border trying to hold on in the face of people using it as a park. There was no easy way in, and he eventually was able to pull up alongside the shoreline and clumsily climb out of the boat. He thought for a moment about keeping the craft there, in case he needed it to escape but as he considered this he felt there had to be a better mode of transportation for getting off his rock, even if it meant swimming for it, and so he cast the kayak adrift.

He scanned the horizon where Tindra was making her way around the point and out into the open ocean, and for one moment, as evening turned to dark, he thought he caught a glimpse of her standing on her board as she disappeared behind the dunes and tall patches of elephant grass. It was enough to put his mind at ease in letting him think she had made it out.

The task facing him wasn't going to be easy, he walked up the steep slope, weaving his way through the tree line, until he was at the edges of Castle Neck and it's parking lot. As he suspected, the lot was filled with law enforcement vehicles, beyond the cars and pickup trucks there were a couple communications rigs, paddy wagons, armored swat, supporting trailers to include a wagon set up with tactical gear, a repair and maintenance station, a few trailers housing bathrooms, and a tow plant generator.

After commandeering the tactical gear, he now felt comfortable enough to infiltrate their basecamp. It wouldn't be difficult for him, he knew their lingo and had monitored their radio transmissions since obtaining the walkie talkie with surveillance ear piece and mic. He knew where to look for information on what they were up to, there would be centralized boards with a layout for what they were trying to achieve, the scheduling of meetings, and plenty of officers milling about discussing what they were trying to accomplish. If Tindra's friends were there he would know soon enough. He made his way over to the generator and opened the side door next to the war switch, there in front of him at eye level, was a small plastic connector. The wires for this ran from the motherboard to the control panel on the back, if after shutting the generator down one loosened that connector just enough so it wouldn't make contact, they wouldn't be able to restart the generator.

Looking around to make sure no one was watching, he had to laugh to himself, the irony of it, no one ever watched a generator that was working. He made his way to the control panel, opened the clear glass pane and grabbed that half-dollar sized dial and switched it to the off position. As the generator sputtered to a halt, he quickly went to the side panel, loosened the connector and closed the door.

Shouts came from all over the lot as the power went out; work lights, trailers, the entire basecamp went dark. Orders were fervently being thrown around, along with cries of frustration and anger. He could hear a group of officers as they gathered to head toward the generator to try and solve the problem. Clive had already made his way well past it and into the darkness of their camp. He looked as if he were a part of the team, but he was part of the chaos, with pistol in hand he was the one who was now cutting a slice from operation poison apple and hoping to give them a little taste of their own medicine.

He couldn't be sure what would happen next, but he was very aware this might be his last chance for doing something right, of being the good guy.

SUP

Tindra had stripped down to her underwear and a small t-shirt. A brisk breeze greeted her head on as she began to paddle out. If she was still feeling tired, the sting of that air had shaken it out of her. It was shocking to her system and awoke her to the process of embarking on her escape.

Her backpack was crammed with everything she could get into it, food items, the purse filled with cash and fake identification cards, and the other essentials she had gotten at the store, it all sat on the nose of her board. This caused Tindra some concern as she worried about capsizing, of losing her balance or being tossed by an ill-timed wave. What little she had left to her name was in that bag. She stood about two-thirds of the way back on the board in wide stance. This allowed her to rock and maintain her balance as she rowed. She practiced with long, slow strokes, rowing on one side and then the other. The glow from the sun was beginning to dim from the fog filled sky, a relentless darkness was seeping out of the East. Ahead of her she could see larger fishing vessels making their way out into the deeper part of the sea, lit up like an alien craft they motored out to farm the ocean for food, their long arms holding the nets that would capture whatever was left in those once plentiful waters. Clive might be right; no one was going to give her a second glance looking like a recreational paddleboarder, even if it was at night.

When she first embarked, she would look over her shoulder to see if she could still see Clive paddle his kayak to the other side of the Ipswich River. Somehow, she was able to watch him until he abandoned his kayak and disappeared along the shoreline. He seemed to have some strange underlying grasp of this mad, jaded, upside-down world. Perhaps it was the fact he was so much more involved with it, or maybe more acceptant of it. She had always thought of herself as cynical, or at least having a streak of cynicism to help keep things in check, to maintain her balance in the face of society's ills. Everyday though, she was awakening to the fact that those who ran things were simply uncaring, the decisions they were making affected so many people, and at the core of these decisions they weren't looking out for the best interest of anyone but themselves. The thought process for laying this all out seemed stark, absolute, and with no way for an individual to ever get back to a stable footing.

Once a thing like civility leaves politics, nothing good can come of it, arguments of compromise being a sign of weakness is soon to follow, until all that is left is bitter partisanship and a divide. Much like the bathwater going down the drain once the plug has been pulled, all that is left are the dirt and stains of its usage. That's why the system was beyond repair, there seemed to be no way to ever bring things back to a place of normalcy. It was like those nuclear reactors that went catastrophic, when they finally dumped their cores it was a toxic waste site that spilled out far beyond control, taking decades to clean, and all the while it would hurt, it would injure, and it would kill. Everyone was on their own, to be disbelieved, exploited, stripped of every ounce of dignity and left to rot in the politically radioactive environment. These real and grotesque thoughts were making it a lot easier for Tindra to paddle away.

As she rowed, the ocean turned dark and choppy, as its waters looked to be pumped from some black ominous abyss. Besides the tsunami walls, there were no real guide points, nothing along the horizon of that ocean a traveler could lock onto in hopes of making it. The only things that looked to be welcoming her were the lights from houses beyond the rolling dunes of sand and tall grass, and to do that she would have to paddle back from where she came, and she just wasn't ever going to do that. Before long she began to pass through a heavier mist, its cold dew continually kissed her skin and caused her to get goosebumps, enveloping her in a cold that could only come from the vast emptiness of the sea. Traces of thick clouds began to form above her, and soon it would all disappear under the heavy blanket of fog. It would only make it more difficult to see the choppy conditions ahead, or where she was bound, or if something out there was coming for her. These unknowns should have frightened her, but this was the world she lived in, slowly being enveloped in fog and darkness, of a future uncertain, and of more endings than new beginnings. One bad break could knock an individual down for months or even years to come with no one there to lend a hand, one wrong move and a person could lose everything, with no one ever shedding a tear or ever really caring. She paddled through it, the backpack on the nose of her board getting wet, her legs cramping from the cold. This should have had her turning toward shore and scuttling her board, doing everything in her power to find another way out, but she kept at it. Too many people had quit on her, but she wasn't a quitter now, and she never would be.

EPILOGUE

They were turning the apartment upside down. The agents were cutting couch cushions open, lifting furniture and turning it over, emptying drawers and cabinets searching for anything of value, fingerprints, a passport, pornography, prescription drugs, letters to a lover, a manifesto, anything that would give them a clearer picture of the fugitive they were now in hot pursuit of.

Castle Neck was a complete disaster and because of it they were embarrassed. It was a colossal failure with the headlines in the press reading; *Poison Apple puts Agents to Sleep.* No one in the Maryland Procurement Office was very happy about the leak that pointed to them being there and tried distancing themselves as much as possible, pinning the failure on local law enforcement, an agent gone rogue, or a faulty generator. One of the directors actually promised the agency would step in with its seemingly unlimited resources and clean things up, this was a bold promise that had everyone involved motivated for finding the members of Persona Non Grata. It was this energy and purpose that brought them down into Tindra's apartment and had them thoroughly going through her effects.

One of these agents was in the bedroom snooping around, carefully lifting and looking under things before they came in and began tearing the room apart.

Searching around her bed, the agent noticed a large Moleskine notebook. He pulled it from its resting spot, lodged between the mattress and the frame, and opened it to find he was holding Tindra's journal. He slowly walked out of the room reading it as a few more agents went into her bedroom to see what they could find. The agent reading her journal found a chair and turned it upright so he could sit in it, continuing to read as her apartment was ruthlessly ransacked for more clues about her enigmatic life.

Novels by
R. Vincent Tibbetts

Red Planet Pioneer

The year is 2079 and colonizing Mars is about to become a very dangerous business. Corporations are the drivers of a process that governments desperately want to regulate. Investors expect massive profits from taking such risks. With the world teetering on global catastrophe, Xavier Pentagrass has been sent to Mars to run the Red Planet Pioneer Corporation. As all are about to find out it will soon become his personal cause.

The technology driving the colonization process is the development of a new android race known as Dextoids. Breakthroughs in quantum computing have allowed for their manifestation. Humanity has grown to rely upon these creations for every single facet of their existence.

Out in the barren plains of Mars two Dextoids have escaped their minders. Their extensive knowledge can't prepare them for freedom. Unhinged from humanity, they will shape the attitude for how the Red Planet will be colonized, and how mankind will treat the Dextoid population for years to come.

A genetically engineered adventure, welcome to Red Planet Pioneer.

Siege Engines

An Empire intent on flexing its power as an elite vessel plunges itself into the unknown, and all of it, pinned on a rescue of frail hope

None would ever question the fact that deep space travel is a dirty business. Interplanetary trade is the driver for conquering new worlds and is the reason the

Empire intends to colonize the galactic arm. No one stood in their way until they began picking up a distress signal from one of their own.

The Champollion was bathed in technology that was nothing short of state of the art. Its crew was handpicked to aid in the journey of exploration, and with Rutherford as their Captain, the Empire trusted them implicitly to expand their spatial bounds — until they went too far.

A space opera that weaves in and out of repressed worlds and the controlling tentacles of the Empire, of fear and the fearless, and of one women who must rise to the occasion and find a way to 'put it on the strength.'

The powerful have something to fear.

The Descent from Anvil

On a world where the days are ticking toward extinction, the desperate inhabitants send their best emissaries into the unknown for a solution.

Coiled in the distrust of the Cold War and faced with an enigma that threatens humanity, three ordinary people wage an extraordinary fight to bridge the fissure between worlds to save a people they cannot comprehend. Every action they take ripples through time in a macabre dance of destiny and determination.

The Concierge

Marteen lives in a world where strict cultural change moves at a slow and steady pace in one ominous direction. Those who can find connection with the wealthy and powerful are rewarded, and it's difficult to see how one can achieve any headway without brushing elbows with the elite, but Marteen has a loose plan to succeed in this top-heavy society. There is one job within the confines of the metropolis that seems to place him at the center of this ideological hub—but is a complete mystery on how he can attain it, and that is the job of the concierge.

Determined to achieve his goal, Marteen embarks on a journey that will open his eyes to the world around him, all the while plunging him headlong toward his aim. Welcome to the arcane and obscure world of the concierge

R. Vincent Tibbetts was raised in Western Pennsylvania during the 1970's. It was a time when their professional football team captured the heart of a city. It was because of this that the surrounding areas immersed itself in a culture of winning, however those feelings changed with the death of the steel industry. Witnessing the economic shockwave ripple through these communities from the gutting of such an industrial expanse had an impact on his psyche. It led him to see his surroundings in a new light, he grew to have an appreciation for how things worked, the workings of the natural world, and developing a mindset for conservation.

His interests in art, photography, and film production brought him to California and a career in the entertainment business where he is a Chief Lighting Technician and Studio Electrician.

He is an entrepreneur at heart.

His hobbies include beach volleyball, softball, golf, hiking, camping, and surfing.

He resides in Long Beach, California.